She Set Him Up

She Set Him Up

Whitney Love

Copyright © 2024 Whitney Love

The moral right of the author has been asserted.

Apart from any fair dealing for the purposes of research or private study, or criticism or review, as permitted under the Copyright, Designs and Patents Act 1988, this publication may only be reproduced, stored or transmitted, in any form or by any means, with the prior permission in writing of the publishers, or in the case of reprographic reproduction in accordance with the terms of licences issued by the Copyright Licensing Agency. Enquiries concerning reproduction outside those terms should be sent to the publishers.

This is a work of fiction. Names, characters, businesses, places, events and incidents are either the products of the author's imagination or used in a fictitious manner. Any resemblance to actual persons, living or dead, or actual events is purely coincidental.

Matador
Unit E2 Airfield Business Park,
Harrison Road, Market Harborough,
Leicestershire. LE16 7UL
Tel: 0116 2792299
Email: books@troubador.co.uk
Web: www.troubador.co.uk/matador
Twitter: @matadorbooks

ISBN 978 1805141 297

British Library Cataloguing in Publication Data.
A catalogue record for this book is available from the British Library.

Printed and bound in Great Britain by 4edge Limited
Typeset in 11pt Minion Pro by Troubador Publishing Ltd, Leicester, UK

Matador is an imprint of Troubador Publishing Ltd

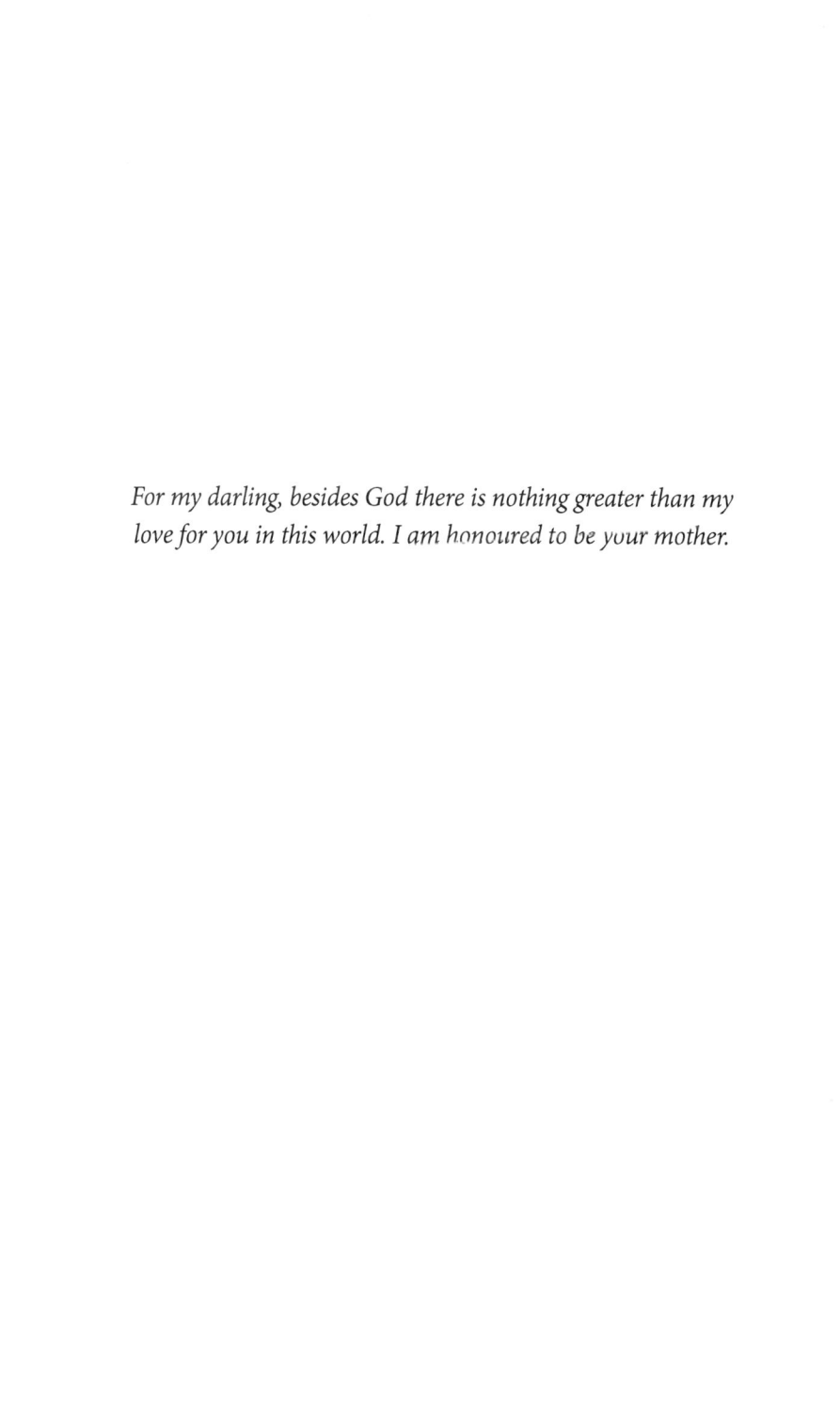

For my darling, besides God there is nothing greater than my love for you in this world. I am honoured to be your mother.

Contents

Introduction		ix
1	My blueprint	1
2	A child where?	20
3	When I grow up	48
4	Sitting with fear and regret	57
5	Punching above my weight	64
6	Seasons change	94
7	Guilt	133
8	The arrival	148

Introduction

My pregnancy came about against the odds and was unwelcomed by my child's father and his family. Raising a child alone is daunting, fraught with stigma and sometimes unbearable hardship, but that is exactly what I chose to do.

For many years I have heard echoes of 'she set him up' coming from a man who felt played by a woman over a pregnancy he did not want. Those echo chambers where men assemble – online, in barber shops or on high streets and such – to ruminate out loud like bands of reluctant fathers, often sound like wave after wave of sweeping judgements against the women they have had sexual relations with. All this from men who, often, had willingly made their bed but didn't want to lie in it.

Throughout my life I had never fully grasped how deeply troubling, confusing and painful these situations could be. But when my own fertility was called into *serious* doubt my understanding deepened.

Suddenly, *I* was labelled as the girl who 'set him up'. And all at once, it was indeed deeply troubling, confusing and painful.

Before we get into the meat and bones of all that, I revisit the memories and unfold the defining moments that have been the measure of me and my life before 'she set him up' became personal. And I invite you to peel back the layers of my story; use discernment to explore the choices, people and events that led me here, to single motherhood.

In *She Set Him Up*, I try to lay down a blueprint of my life to not only tell the stories of my life but to provide a platform for all people – particularly women – to tell their story. To anyone who feels unseen, misunderstood or unheard, please draw closer, gather around in the spaces between the sentences on these pages and lay your truth bare. Every single one of us has a heartache we need to unburden ourselves from. I implore you to set yours down on the ground.

The only way we can ever hope to learn or help each other is by sharing our stories. Things are rarely as black and white as they first appear. With several twists and turns, *She Set Him Up* creates an open forum for discussion around topics that are still taboo.

I am optimistic that by the end of this introspective book, you will re-examine your own life experiences to make sense of how they have shaped you.

In the stakes of love and sex, truth and familial relations, the highs are high, and the lows are lonely. That much will be true in anyone's story. But this right here, written in these lines, is my story. This happened to me. This is where I came from, and here is where I begin.

One

My blueprint

I peel one eye open to glance at the time on my phone – it's 3am. Since midnight, I've been lying in bed – half asleep and half awake – beneath the light of the moon.

I sigh in frustration. My mind refuses to rest; instead, it churns around like a well-oiled machine replaying conversations that continue to plague me.

My pregnancy pillow provides limited comfort as I close my eyes and try to sleep just as you're kicking from inside my womb. You remind me that it is not just me alone with my thoughts; it is us, and you will be here soon.

*

It may seem contrary to say that for many years I never wanted a child. My early life experiences rewired me into believing that bringing a child into this world was a bad idea.

I grew up in South London; the girls I saw having

babies were young mums struggling, living in social housing and on benefits.

I had been a product of a single mother. We, too, had lived in social housing. My mother always had to work and to not – as she saw it – take handouts.

My mother would always say, "Don't beg, don't steal and don't borrow." And that was the compass by which she tried to live and encouraged the same of me.

I have called my mother by her first name – Esther – for as long as I can remember. I recall the first time it was acknowledged. It had obviously tickled her because she laughed from her stomach, a full belly laugh, before responding with, "You're too fresh!"

Life was not easy for Esther. Even from my childhood perspective I understood enough to know that things were at times strained and I needed to lighten the load by helping.

I don't think Esther ever said explicitly that I had to do tasks to help, but I do believe there was an unwritten rule between us; I just knew what needed to be done.

While Esther went to work as a nurse I would stay home alone. "Don't open the door to no one, you hear me?" she would warn.

"Yes, Mum," I would reply using the proper title. I knew by her tone that this was important and that there was no time for 'foolishness' by way of calling her Esther.

Once she left the house, I would make myself busy by cleaning it from top to bottom. I would put the dirty clothes in the washing machine and use the wash cycle time to start preparing dinner. By the time Esther returned home there was nothing left for her to do.

During that period, I could not have been more than six years old. When I reflect on the average six-year-olds today, the contrast could not be more marked.

Esther and I worked well as a team. I was proud of us. With time, my assistance afforded me fun opportunities like attending a Saturday school for lessons in ballet, tap, modern dance and drama.

There may have been other single parents that also took their children to Saturday school, but I did not know of any. All my friends came from two-parent homes with a mum and dad who were married.

Back then, and perhaps even now, I would say it was unusual for a black child to be allowed to have sleepovers at their friend's house, but I was allowed to on several occasions. I am grateful to Esther for giving me those moments; they meant a lot to me. Those sleepovers are a significant reason for some of the happy memories I have of my childhood. Perhaps unintentionally, they showed me something I could aspire to, a snapshot of how families were supposed to be when at their best.

One of my fondest memories is being sat round the dinner table of my friend Hannah's house; we sat together with her mum, dad and brother Josh to a massive serving of my favourite meal: macaroni cheese. Hannah and I spent the whole meal laughing and giggling. So much so that I was unable to control my fits of laughter about goodness knows what. The jovial eruption of giggles made the macaroni that I had in my mouth fly right out and find its way onto Hannah's dad's plate. I was mortified. I stopped laughing immediately and held my breath in shock and anticipation. But no one flinched or seemed bothered at all.

The definite scolding that I was expecting never came. No one skipped a beat or paused to acknowledge what happened. It was as if they hadn't even noticed. I recall my amazement that the adults were just happy and very chilled out about our childish shenanigans. That was a breath of fresh air to me.

By comparison, had I been at home with my dad present (I'll get into how he arrived in my life a little later) and that happened, it would have been a completely different story.

In moments like that where I had experienced a stark contrast to how things were in my home, I began to idealise being a member of a different family. And for me, because the only positive experiences that I had to draw upon were of my white friends, I began to wish that a white family would adopt me.

I have never openly confessed this to anyone, but it was something I held on to for as long as I can remember.

As an adult I now know that you can have good or bad families irrespective of race, colour or creed. But as a child, most of my friends were white, English and middle class. They were the only real-life examples I had to compare my family to.

Esther and I lived in Dulwich, I was the only black child amongst my white friends, but there was never any feeling of being different. We were just being. All of us were so perfectly innocent and happy to play and enjoy each other's company.

Esther had brought me up to be a respectful child who went to church every Sunday. She was from a French-speaking island in the Caribbean. The use of proper grammar was of high importance and always emphasised by Esther, as was the need to physically present myself in a respectable way.

Our clothes were always clean and freshly pressed. Face and body creamed, hair oiled.

I was a bookworm who was well spoken and had quite a large vocabulary for a young child. Esther played a huge part in that because she would ensure that she spoke to me without babying me, in an adult yet child-appropriate way.

Esther felt it was more useful for me to be well spoken in the English language and focus on expanding my vocabulary. Although she spoke to me in French creole, she never made a habit of it and would do so sparingly.

Esther was born in the warm sun of the Caribbean and had quite a middle-class upbringing, where she attended an Anglican school. That education was funded by the Anglican church in England and the educational standard was that of a grammar school in England.

Our family were well known on the island. They had obtained good social standing, owning their own home which they built to their specification.

In those days – the 1950s – it was quite common to be raised by grandparents or aunts and uncles; life was no different for Esther.

She had a happy childhood, surrounded by lots of family, with land that was plentiful and fruitful. You could live off the food on their land. And that's exactly what the family did.

They had everything growing on the land, from breadfruit to plantains; they never wanted for anything.

Esther's mother, my Grandma Charlotte, had immigrated to England in the hope of setting up her career as a nurse.

It was common practice that a family member would go to England in pursuit of a better life for their family. What was also common practice was to send money back home to the family, to help build the wealth and lifestyles of those in the Caribbean.

If people who came to Britain in search of prosperity did not already have land or property back home, they would save from the money they made in Britain to put towards building a house back in the Caribbean.

Grandma Charlotte's main agenda was to set up a life for her and Esther in England. Soon enough, she had set herself up sufficiently and sent for Esther to come and live with her.

Grandma Charlotte had also been a single parent. I am not sure how much of that had been by choice, but I do know that her family did not like Esther's father. And Grandma Charlotte honoured her family by cutting all ties with him.

From the stories I was told about my Grandma Charlotte, it was clear to me she was not average – she was a special woman. With the support of her large family, who all lived together like *The Waltons*, she began to carve out her own independence with a goal to migrate to England where she imagined the streets were paved with gold. Grandma Charlotte was multi-skilled. By the time she was set for England, she had secretarial skills and was an excellent seamstress and a qualified midwife. And though I never got to meet her because she fell victim to cancer at the young age of forty, I know that she was a very cool Grandma who owned and rode a Vespa motorcycle no less.

Esther was nine years old when Grandma Charlotte sent for her, and she left the Caribbean to live in England. Sadly, it was not long after she arrived that Grandma Charlotte died from cancer. All at once, Esther found herself alone, an orphan far from home in a place she barely knew.

Despite her grief, through the years, Esther was determined to pay homage to her mother in one way or another. She worked hard to study and gain qualifications to become a nurse. Of all the things that can be passed down through the bloodline, I am grateful Grandma Charlotte strong will was passed onto Esther and subsequently onto me.

But life can continue to be cruel sometimes. The torment it dishes out can be so harsh. Because of the grief of losing her mother at such a young and impressionable age, with no close relatives in England to tend to her brokenness, some years later Esther suffered a breakdown.

From then onwards, the shadow of illness would descend over her and cause multiple breakdowns that rendered her useless to herself and to me for long periods of time.

During those periods, Esther had to spend some time in what she called 'the mental institution' – a large London psychiatric hospital.

Watching your mother deteriorate right in front of your eyes is one of the hardest things a child could go through. Esther would turn into someone I no longer recognised and could no longer accept as my mother. It was confusing and soul-destroying. Bearing witness to this illness up close and personal, I learned quickly that all the things she said she could see and hear and would point and stare and respond to, only existed inside her imagination.

I remember a time when Esther's illness took hold of both of us during a night that felt like the longest night ever. It is a night that haunts me, even now.

I had gone to sleep in Esther's bed with her as I so often did. I had taken to sleeping in the bed with Esther because I was afraid of the dark. I was afraid of the monsters that could be hiding within the shadows in my room. But now, instead of the safety and comfort that I longed for, I found myself wide awake inside a nightmare, not knowing if my next breath would be my last.

The extra body heat made things feel cosy. I liked putting my feet up on Esther's hip – as though it was a footstool – when she lay on her side in the foetal position. It felt so comfortable, at least for me. And no matter how much she complained, somehow my little feet found their way back to the same position to rest on the dip of her hip. I wiggled my toes in comfort and quietly giggled to myself victoriously until I slipped into sleep.

*

There are moments in life that leave you with a distinct feeling of inevitability in your bones about the things that are passed on through the bloodline. These unseen things create patterns which repeat themselves throughout generations.

Here I am – with my mother's shoe's firmly on my feet – a single mother.

Day and night I weave through the steep learning curve of looking after a small child alone; it's mind-blowing and exhausting all at once. In a restful moment when you are sound asleep and I am – of course – wide awake, I smile as I notice you become the child I used to be. Your tiny feet have found themselves upon the nook of my hip just as mine used to with Essie. For the first time I empathise with how Essie must have felt on those nights all those years ago with my feet lodged in her hip. Nevertheless, I am assured that you are as happy as I used to be in those moments and everything *feels worth it.*

*

Sound asleep, I was snapped back awake by the sound of desperate screams. "Help! Help! Somebody help us – someone is trying to break in and kill us!" The screams were so harrowing that my eyes flicked wide open and I jumped right out of my skin. For a moment my vision was blurry, but then it sharpened to focus on the figure I could see a few feet away. It was Esther, leaning out of the open bedroom window in her long, white and flowy nightdress that was billowing in the wind like a ghost. My heart was beating faster and louder. I was terrified.

My body tensed and my little feet curled. I balled my fists and gripped the sheets, pulling them closer for comfort. But comfort would not come. Within a few seconds my nightclothes were damp with sweat, but then, just as suddenly as it had begun, Esther's screaming stopped.

She calmly turned around from the window as though

there was nothing left to be done. As her eyes met mine, she said nonchalantly, "Oh, you're awake." She turned on her heels, briskly walked over and sat beside me on the bed. Looking straight into my eyes she said, "They're trying to kill us." Her words stopped my breath for what felt like an eternity.

Esther's words were so visceral, they crawled around under my skin.

I froze as scattered thoughts continued to spin around and around my head. I noticed I was shaking when my teeth began to chatter. I wished I was dreaming.

Bang! Bang! Bang! This was real. I could hear the thuds at the door and see the door rattle then settle back into place. This wasn't a figment of Esther's imagination. For the first time I, too, could see and hear everything Esther could see and hear. "You see, you didn't believe me, did you? I'm not mad," she said.

Then, the door stopped rattling. Esther and I huddled on the bed with only silence between us.

And then, *bang! Bang!* "This is the police," I heard a man say alongside the crackling of his radio. I let out an audible sigh of relief.

The rest of that night is a blur. But the police did confirm they found no signs of forced entry. How can I explain what I saw and heard that night? The door, the banging. Perhaps they were nothing more than a hallucination resulting from the extreme stress of witnessing Esther's outburst and tapping into her fear. I wonder whether I, too, could become ill just like Esther. That thought terrifies me. I reason with myself and concede the hallucinating was a one-off incident that had occurred under duress. And I have tried to bury it in the deepest corner of my mind.

I have drawn the conclusion that there is a stark difference between Esther and me in terms of our approach to mental health. I am open to help should I need it. I sought help during my own depressive episode that occurred many years later. Esther, on the other hand, was undeniably anti anyone who would even dare question she was anything but in her right mind.

The events of that distressing night prompted me to make conscious decisions during my formative years to never do anything that might trigger the onset of my own mental health negatively. I chose to stay away from recreational drugs and frowned heavily upon those who partook. With age and some wisdom, I now appreciate that it is the choice of every individual to choose their own path without the weight of my judgement. Nonetheless, I do have a strong belief that drugs can trigger this illness that is in my blood. And I would do anything to avoid awakening that beast.

The extremities of mental health, when on a downward slope can be an upsetting illness to see play out or be exposed to. It can lead people to mock you or withdraw from you completely because they find the Jekyll and Hyde of it too much emotionally to bear. I am ashamed to say that the latter is true of Esther and me.

I deeply regret that things have become as distant as they are between us. But I have resigned myself, after years of heavy trauma from Esther's deteriorated health ebbing away at my spirit, that it was either her or me. Knowing how vulnerable I feel around Esther, I have made a conscious decision to place my health above hers. I am grateful that I am still of sound mind. My objective is to preserve my mind by every means necessary, even at the detriment of my relationship with Esther.

Honestly speaking, during my youth there were publicly distressing situations that would occur that corroded any confidence I had left to safely maintain a good relationship with Esther.

At the age of fifteen I got my first job; I worked at McDonald's in Leicester Square, London. I was such a diligent worker and proud of my efforts to make my own money. Back then, I was still hopelessly naive enough to believe that I could effectively manage Esther's illness. Although she had open access to me, in as far as knowing where I worked and having the phone number to my job, I just needed to ensure I maintained a healthy distance so that boundaries were not crossed.

Esther's ill health sometimes made her erratic and obsessive. It would not be unusual for her to call me ten or more times a day and fill the entire voicemail capacity on my mobile with messages. It was suffocating. Whatever means of contact she had, she would thoroughly abuse.

One day, I was at work and overheard two managers talking quietly, or so they thought. They attempted to speak under their breath about the enormous number of times Esther was calling the office to speak to me. Worse still, I heard one of them say, "I think she's mad." Their words killed me. Still, I tried to busy myself with a task nearby to hear a little more of their conversation. I should have known better and just walked away, but I couldn't help myself. I needed to hear everything they were saying.

The managers had concluded that Esther had called one too many times and they were now considering changing the office number. That had to be bad, right?

My breaths became shorter and sharper in disbelief that Esther's illness had spilled over into my work environment. My ears began to burn; my eyes filled up with tears that spilled down my face. To conceal my upset, I quickly brushed the tears away with the back of my hand and tried to continue as though nothing was wrong. I bit down on my tongue, not hard enough to draw blood but hard enough to override the sadness with acute pain. I ordered my tears to dry up and the anxiety lump that was rising in my throat to dissipate. Although I felt the sharp pain I had inflicted on myself, I knew that the sting on my tongue would eventually fade. And I took comfort in the fact that I had managed to compose myself.

After that incident I knew I could never allow Esther to intrude in my workspaces again. When I left that job to work elsewhere, she was not granted any work contact information.

You see, with each time that Esther reminded me in some way that she was unwell and her illness infringed upon my world, I felt I had no choice but to distance myself. I have continued to disallow her from one form of direct access to me or another. And after four decades our only means of communication has been reduced to emails.

Though my relationship with Esther is clearly fragmented, it will never detract from the fact that I will always long for a mother. I have had to accept that it is not within Esther's capabilities. But I can still dream. And I often do.

Admittedly there have been times that I have felt ashamed of Esther's illness, particularly when growing up. What other people think means so much more when you're young and impressionable. Like so many people, I was trying to discover who I was and all I wanted to do was fit in. But my exposure to her illness prevented that to a degree.

I have seen myself as a misfit for as long as I can remember. But it was the secrets of my family home which I kept for the longest time that made me more guarded with people. The question loomed: who could I trust with all that was going on within the walls of my home? *There must be some people who are trustworthy, right?* I thought. But Esther's voice would ring louder inside my head, insisting that people could not be trusted and would only take advantage of me.

As I understood it, Esther's chain of thoughts were a combination of her illness and her grief that were expressed through her mistrust of people. So, over the years, I have trained my mind as much as possible, to take what she said with a pinch of salt. I remind myself that if I allow myself to get tangled into her way of thinking, I would be exposing myself as more vulnerable to her illness and encouraging it to take over me too.

My greatest wish has always been that I could fix Esther. And though I understand this is beyond my reach, it still binds me up inside. I feel both helpless and useless that I cannot make it better. My soul feels persecuted constantly from knowing that I have a mum but understanding that I don't *really* have a mum.

For every Mother's Day and significant family calendar event that I am without a fully able mother I feel so alone in the world. I have always judged myself harshly for feeling like this. I believe that when people see I have no immediate family around and exist just in and of myself, they must wonder what I could have done for this to have happened. They must think I'm an awful person, rotten to the core, for no immediate family to actively be a part of my life, right? I am ashamed of the fact that for the most part, I am alone.

Isn't it funny how the thing you lack is the one thing you yearn for most? You could have everything else in the whole world yet still be concentrating on that one missing thing. It creates this void of discontent inside oneself. But you may not always attribute this emotional low to what it really is: the loss of what never was. I have never blamed anyone for how I feel because when you are feeling tender it is often difficult to see beyond yourself and your situation. But every now and then when I see families existing happily together, I cannot help but pity myself for not being a part of a unit. Safe and secure, happy and loved. But alas, I can only play the cards that I have been dealt, right?

Where do you put the love that you possess inside when you have nobody to share it with who accepts you though you do not belong? I know myself to be a loving person, yet the love stored within me feels forever unrequited. You cannot beg or buy your way into love. Perhaps it is a membership given at birth that is activated by the true love of another somebody like you, more of those connections help one feel like less of an outsider.

Finding that connection is not guaranteed. Finding that connection can often take a lifetime.

I have often pondered what would happen if something happened to me. What if I was to curl up in a ball of pain or gorge out my eyes, would anyone notice or care? Or would that sorry scenario play out like the scene straight out of *Bridget Jones's Diary*, with no messages from a single concerned soul, ironically, not even from my mother. What a shame and a huge waste for any human existence. We were never made to be alone. No human should be an island. At least, not for too long.

If a genie could have presented itself to me in the moments before Esther would relapse, I would have asked for a cure. All I wanted as a little girl was my mummy to be whole and not the tormented pieces that she became. In primary school, I would study the encyclopaedia and learn about the moon and its effects on mental health, hoping that I would discover something significant enough to make her better. But I never discovered that something. I have never known a feeling quite like the disappointment of that.

At the tail end of the eighties and early nineties, the attitudes towards mental illness were despicable.

Back then, every way people and facilities dealt with mental health felt cold and inhumane. In general, people were extremely unkind and cutting with the terminology they casually used towards it.

"Essie (as her family called Esther) is mad," they would say. And just like that, you were a reject of society, dispelled and spewed right out of its mouth into the great abyss of shit. Facilities and attitudes are getting better – painstakingly slowly.

The knock-on impact that these episodes had on me meant that, during Esther's relapses, I had to go into foster care.

Like a ragdoll being ejected from a reject bin, I would then be tossed into the home of a perfect stranger until she recovered.

I'm not sure what scared me more as a child seeing Esther's mental health deteriorate, or going to a stranger's house whom I would feel awkward with and unsure of how they wanted me to be. Could I be heard and seen? Or just seen and not heard?

But as uncomfortable as those temporary changes were, I think it was necessary not only for Esther to recover but also for me to have respite from the trauma of her illness.

It also gave me another glimpse into other families' lives. I saw different ways of caring, other expressions of love that were sadly lacking in my home.

One lady who looked after me for a brief time had a son of similar age to me. They were a family of three: mum, dad and son. I got on well with her son; we were just children, so we played well. Of course, sometimes we fought, but for the most part we made good playmates. This lady stood out to me from the catalogue of people I had stayed with because she made a conscious effort to relate to me in a small but significant way. She told me that once upon a time, she too had been in care. That was a beautiful moment of shared vulnerability that meant so much to me. I appreciated the fact that she was trying to relate to me but more so the fact that she completely understood. Perhaps it was her way of telling me that there was nothing wrong with me and none of this was my fault. Of all the homes that I stayed in, hers is one of the fondest memories because of that simple act of empathy. If she were reading this book and recognising herself in this story, I would tell her, "Thank you."

Of an evening her and her husband would take a bath together as her son and I played. The bathroom door would be ajar, so we could all see each other. The strangest thing to me was, though I had never seen a woman and a man take a bath together, nothing about it felt uncomfortable or unnatural; it just fitted perfectly into the bubble of love their home provided.

When it was finally time to be returned back to Esther because she was better, I distinctly remember a part of me that was sad to say goodbye. I was a mixed bag of emotions. Although I was thrilled Esther was better and I could go back home to her, I had enjoyed my time with this family and perhaps there was a part of me that wasn't quite ready for it to end. I felt uncomfortable about feeling so contrary. Inside it pained me because perhaps it meant I was betraying Esther by enjoying another woman being a mother in her place.

I guess the upside of all the upheaval and movement from home to home is that I have learnt to survive no matter what happens. It has taught me that the most crucial thing of all is to adapt. Without the ability to adapt at any given moment, you can be rendered useless to yourself and others and can easily remain stuck and adrift from the progress that is meant for you.

*

After emptying my bladder for the hundredth time, I admit defeat to the words spinning inside my head and kiss sleep goodbye. I abandon the bed and settle into my rocking chair. I try not to think about all the long, sleepless nights ahead of me as I lift each leg slowly onto the footrest and rock myself back and forth. Gently stroking my stomach, I try to fill my head with only thoughts of you; my little one, you are worth every mountain that I will have to climb.

Two

A child where?

I have reached my second trimester and I'm so tired. I feel as though I am sleeping with my eyes wide open.

Tired does not seem like a big enough word to convey the tiredness I feel; this is the most tired I've ever felt in my life. My body feels as heavy as lead. My mind feels full of junk and harsh words that have imprinted themselves onto me.

What kind of mother will I be to you – my precious miracle? I am terrified of becoming the embodiment of the parents I have tried so hard not to be.

My life has been missing you. Every fibre of my being wants you and loves you but is yet to believe that I deserve you. The circumstances surrounding you and I feel both cruel and crippling.

It's hard not to tear myself apart when this low mood won't leave me alone. But I have got to get through this and reckon with the almost unbearable weight of how I came to be your mother. I am aware and beyond humbled that God has chosen to knit you together in my womb. I close my eyes and say a little prayer for us.

*

I can pull on pleasant memories from my childhood, but I also understand the pressures of being a single mother and, in turn, what that meant for a child who was a product of that.

You see, life was hard because there was only one adult, which meant that for me as a child, I had to grow up quickly. I had to shoulder some of the burden to reduce the weight of responsibility on Esther.

Once I was old enough to get a part-time job while studying at college, things didn't ease. I long understood that Esther needed a mother. Whenever she felt vulnerable or had the ridiculous notion that she no longer needed her medication, there I was mothering her, guiding her through life.

For many years I had been an only child; it had been just Esther and me. But fourteen years later, she had my baby brother.

A few years before my brother was born, Esther had gone on a soul-searching mission. It must have been eating away at her all those years, not knowing her own father. It was not until she was an adult in her thirties that she decided to find him. Considering there was no social media, it did not take long for her to unpick the clues from years of careless whispers to solve the mystery of her father back home in the Caribbean.

I remember us flying to my mother's homeland; I also remember feeling disgruntled about the fact that, although it was my six-week summer holiday off school, I was told I would be attending school in the Caribbean during that period and – according to Esther – that would be a good experience for me.

Once we arrived, my eyes were opened to a new way of life. That was the first time I had ever experienced a black society, country or world. All the people were melanin rich just like me; there was every shade of brown skin glowing under the sun and I felt like a 'melaninaire'. The climate was so warm and humid, where you did not sweat profusely but rather your skin felt sun-kissed and clammy to touch. There was a pleasant feeling in the air, a feeling of relaxation and no need to worry, good vibes. It was not so much about the excitement of being somewhere different, but more about the freeing wave that comes over you just by being somewhere other than home.

The perception of time for a child differs vastly from that of an adult. It's not unusual as an adult to feel like time just slips through our fingers so quickly, but for me back then, time felt so endless. I instantly did away with my plan to count down the days until I returned home.

The Island had a distinctive scent in the air that could cling to your skin like perfume. If I could taste it, I am sure it would taste sweet. I loved eating cultural foods that I was familiar with but which tasted so much better there because they were fresher. I suppose the sunshine, the blue skies and the ocean will always make everything more amazing.

A few days into our trip I was taken to the local school

and introduced to the headmistress. I was then put into the classes according to my age; I quickly understood that even though I looked just like everyone else, they did not see me as one of them.

I found this to have its perks. You see, although I too was black, I was a special classification of black – I was 'English' as they referred to me. This classification meant that although I may have got a question or two wrong in class, I did not receive the same treatment as the other children. No, I was spared the rod – or should I say the ruler, quite literally. I watched on in shock as I saw my classmates being slapped on the hand with a ruler for answering a question wrong.

I quickly became accustomed to seeing these methods of discipline, so much so that it began to amuse me. Not because it was funny, but because I realised that being 'English' gave me automatic privileges that meant I was untouchable.

My other memories of schooling were that, although the classrooms had basic decor and resources, the children were advanced with top-tier knowledge that would put children in England to shame. Perhaps the swift threat of the ruler had its advantages and made the children's willingness to learn much greater.

My fondest memory of schooling there was that I was quite the social butterfly. Because I was different, everyone wanted to get to know me. To this day, Esther has never let me forget that each day she came to collect me from school I had a different boy on my arm.

The day Esther had been waiting for finally came. This was it; she had done it – she had found her father and we were going to meet him. The consequences of which, I would later fall prey to.

This was the first grandparent I had met, and I am honestly not sure I was moved in any direction. I was used to the dynamic between Esther and me, quite content aside from the disruptions of her illness. I did not feel like I was missing the absence of anything or anybody at all.

That said, my grandfather seemed like a genuinely nice man. He had kind eyes and a warm radiance that encompassed him that was different from the heat of the Caribbean sun. He was an open book with his thoughts and feelings.

To me it seemed that should he be struck dead in that very moment, he would die a happy man because he had finally met his long-lost daughter. I guess the cherry on top was me, his grandchild.

"She'll go far," he said. "You make sure no harm comes to her and she'll do well in life," he commented, as though he possessed a gift of seeing far into the future and knowing the trouble that lay ahead.

The connection that Esther had made with her father awakened a need within her for me – she no longer wanted me to grow up without knowing my own father. Esther was determined to break this cycle of the absent father once and for all and introduce me to mine.

There was a notable difference in Esther after she met her father. She seemed more confident and purpose driven.

Before meeting her father, she must have wondered so many things: what he was like as a person, what he looked like and why he had not been around. Now she had met him, she must have felt fulfilled to know him and know she had an extra branch of family that she so desperately needed. Once she had made that first connection, she was then able to connect to other branches of her father's tree, namely a sister.

Though this sister lived in America, they struck up a real friendship and it was nice for me to see what those interactions did for her. I could tell Esther felt a part of something bigger than herself. Because, although they were there for her, she had never felt fully loved by her mother's side of the family, so the bond she was developing with her father's side was important. Now she mattered to someone other than me. Although these new family links were distant, they were heartfelt.

With the happiness this extension of family brought her, Esther felt compelled to spread that feeling. She became hell bent on reconnecting with my father so that I too could have the same experience.

It wasn't long after we had returned from our trip that she began making a few calls and enquiries to find my father. Esther knew who he was but had no contact information for him. The one thing that made the task possible was the fact that his brother was famous. This uncle of mine had sung on popular music shows of his time. The only way Esther could reach my father was to go through his brother's management who could pass on a message to my father. So, that is what she did. And then one day, my father turned up.

I will never forget the first impression I had of my father when I met him. He was tall, six foot something, slender in frame but by no means skinny; he was fair skinned just like Ice-T the American rapper. In fact, in many ways to me he was very similar to Ice-T. They both had the same style of goatee beard. A moustache that linked straight into the beard, and just beneath the bottom lip was a pepper of hair. They also both had a mole on their face, but my father's was placed like Marilyn Monroe, neatly above the top of his lip at the far corner.

His style of dress was something I had not observed in any men of his age before; he was suited in a double-breasted blazer and matching trousers, a crisp white shirt and booted in these crocodile patent shiny shoes, and his socks were these silk-embossed, delicate-looking things. For his crown, he wore a trilby hat; his outer garment was a three-quarter-length black coat.

I understood Esther's reasons for introducing him into my life, but I was not very open to it, not that I had any choice.

As far as I was concerned, we were fine, and I did not need him. So, wherever he came from, I wished he would just disappear back to.

Straight away he just seemed to take up occupancy and have opinions which were listened to by Esther. I resented that. How dare he try and assume the role of a father. To me he did not have the right to be my father. Though he had in some small way played a part in making me, it had been almost ten years of non-existence and then suddenly – *boom!* He came bounding in with, 'do as I say'. All I could think was, *I don't think so, mate.*

I could not utter my displeasure, but I could not hide my feelings. I am sure my countenance was pronounced, at least in my head it was. *Why does he have the right to dictate anything pertaining to us when he has not even earnt it?* I asked myself.

The years began to roll by with my father firmly in place with us. When I say with us, I use the term loosely. He did not officially reside with us, but he spent a lot of time in our home. And for the most part, I hated it.

Looking back, I can see why I found this change so hard to deal with. One minute I didn't have a father and the next there was this person in full effect. There had been no thought given to the potential impact of this introduction. One would have thought it might have been a good idea to arrange gradual meetings for the two of us to warm to each other and get to know each other slowly. Instead, he was thrust straight into our lives.

I struggled to get used to the idea of another adult dictating how we did things. Esther and I had been quite close until this point, but the presence of my father had brought about a shift. Hard though it was, I did try to adapt to this change of structure and energy in our home. Despite the raging war within me, I tried to console myself that it wasn't all bad.

Joesph, as Esther called him (it was the pet name she had given him, as though they were playing out characters in the Bible) was an energetic and charismatic man. To get what he wanted, he always had a story to tell about something. And by stories, that is my polite way of saying he was lying. He would tell Esther stories to get her to give him money, all the time. But, to be fair, he would also tell *actual* stories; whether it was about the first black queen of England – Princess Sophia Charlotte, born on 19 May 1744 – or about his personal expeditions to places I had never heard of before, such as Tunbridge Wells and Tahiti. His storytelling broadened my imagination and perception of him having access to high society circles that were a world away from what I knew.

It was all very intriguing. From the wealth of knowledge that he shared, it was clear that he had lived a life far beyond that of the average man.

The expensive taste of Joesph reached far beyond the outwards appearance of his expensive threads; it extended to his recreational habit of smoking rock.

What seemed innocent, accompanying my father to our local sweet shop for a small bottle of still water, a KitKat and a straw, could not have been further from the truth. These items were all going to be used to assemble a pipe for smoking.

On days when he had his poison of choice, he was such a jolly soul. The high-fi would be blaring reggae music, but he would be in Esther's bedroom with the door firmly shut. Neither of us were allowed to go inside.

I had always been disciplined as a child by Esther but nothing more than a smack with a slipper, which was rare. I remember the last time that old slipper made an appearance – it was a short time before my father turned up – on that occasion, it hilariously lost the battle with my hiney by snapping in two.

Now that my father was around, there was a stark contrast in his way of enforcing discipline.

I remember having a diary; I would always put my thoughts and feelings in there. I found it a great outlet of expression. One day, after coming back home from primary school, I carelessly left my diary – that detailed my childhood crush – on the dining table in the front room.

The moment my father picked up my diary and started reading, time slowed down. I felt my heart drop and inside I screamed *noooooo!*

"Who's Alex?" he asked, as though he had not already read the contents of my diary and knew good and well who Alex was.

I tried to keep calm, but I could feel my face burning up and my heart thumping inside my chest ten to the dozen. "Just a boy at school," I replied.

"Didn't I tell you no boys until you're twenty-five?" he snapped back.

"Yes," I responded.

"Yes who?" he barked.

"Yes, sir," I replied in the way he liked to be addressed. But in that moment, it was too little too late to appease him. As soon as I had spoken, everything sped up. All I could see was his fist flying straight towards my face.

My knee jerk reaction had me ducking. And with that, his fist went through the window that was behind me. Worse still, the impact caused some pieces to somehow ricochet and shatter Esther's glass dining table, fragments of which now lay on the carpet like teardrops.

"Ohhh noooo, my table!" Esther pined. In that moment, I knew things would never be the same again.

My heart dropped and I felt a sense of guilt burn through me. I knew the table meant a lot to her; she had worked so hard to buy it. Now look what I had done.

In hindsight I guess I must have felt less important to Esther than her broken table. But what cut deepest was the fact that I never truly felt that she had done all she could to protect me from my father. There were many times when she had physically interjected and got hurt to shield me from my father's blows, but I also have memories of not being able to go into school in case my swelling or bruising raised questions.

At times the house was thick with tension. There was always this build-up in the days waiting for Esther to receive her wages, and he was always aware of that day. He would hang around like a bad smell, waiting for payday with the strong assumption that her money was his.

I would be terrified as she withdrew her funds that if she refused to give it over to him, all hell would break loose. Esther would whisper to me as the three of us walked to the bank; she asked, "Should I give him the money?" The desperation in my eyes would signal that it was best that she did, despite that being the difference between us having food or not.

Sometimes, we were like hostages in our own home, or at least I was. Our home did not feel warm with love for the most part, it was just a house that was a scary place to return to after school. I really wished that she would just stop letting him come around. All she had to do was not let him in anymore, but she could not do it and I could not understand why.

It angered me that she refused to close the door on him as quickly as she had opened it, because, my God, there was every reason to. But she was determined to persevere and so sure that things would eventually turn around and improve. But Esther could not have been more wrong.

Looking back, I know and understand to a degree Esther's reasoning at the time. She was from a certain generation, which did not deem it right to be with any other man than the one who had fathered your children. But I think it ran deeper than that. I think she was scared and had low self-esteem and didn't believe that she could ever be happy with anyone else. I suppose when women get to a certain age, some become despondent and feel like they must accept the man that is stood before them, even if all the signs are as clear as day that he is no good. Perhaps they see themselves in this space of 'last chance saloon' and become more and more accepting of bullshit.

In any other situation I would have admired her willingness to forgive so easily, but she seemed unaware that her forgiveness of him was constantly hurting me. Sadly, only I had the foresight that things were going from bad to worse.

I didn't know what the future held, but it was plain to see that if things continued as they were, the prediction of my grandfather saying, 'she'll go far', would become nothing more than dissipated hopes and dreams.

Having grown up with Esther, I can confidently say that she didn't have a social life. I am not even sure if it ever really crossed her mind that having friends was normal. She was very guarded and mistrusting of others, so it worked for her to keep to a simple routine of work, church and ferrying me to my classes or sleepovers.

Esther wasn't an unfriendly person; on the contrary she was quite warm towards her peers or other parents and those whom we had reason to interact with. But there were few people that I ever saw her truly bond with.

I was her whole life, and she would often say that she had sacrificed so much for me. She had given up on advancing her career because it was important to her to devote her time to me. Perhaps I am being unfeeling and unsympathetic, but to me she was still a nurse, and working as a bank nurse meant that it provided the flexibility that she needed. I wouldn't have minded if she had wanted to work full-time; I was more than happy to go to a childminder or stay home alone.

I would have felt her reference to a sacrifice as a low blow had I the capacity to feel it as it was intended. Instead, I just wondered why on earth she didn't do things that made her happy instead of trying to make me feel bad.

Unfortunately for Esther, I didn't feel bad. I was the child, after all, and hadn't asked to be here.

Looking back, I believe she was trying to reason with me as though I was an adult who would understand her predicament or be able to offer her the sympathy she was clearly looking for. Or perhaps all she really required of me was understanding that she did a lot for us and tried to put my needs above her own. I should have offered verbal gratitude, but I simply listened without responding.

Esther would read the *South London Press* religiously, but I remember one day when she brought the paper home; there was a story inside that obviously struck her as important enough to summon my father from the bedroom to read it with her in our front room. They were both buzzing around it, making hand gestures and shaking their heads in disbelief.

I did not care much for this adult behaviour of important news, but by their body language alone I could tell that they were about to spill; I was about to be brought into the knowledge of this news bulletin.

"Ehhhh ehhhh, Jojo, I can't believe it." Esther gasped.

"Imagine," he replied.

Not long after, Esther glanced at me while my father's head was still stuck in the paper and said, "A black child reported his parents to the police for hitting him. What is this world coming to? You better not do something like that, you hear me."

That, however, was a groundbreaking nugget of information which I held onto. She was right to be shocked at the story; it was unheard of for a black child to ever report their parents. That was not what 'we' did. In my head I saluted this boy child for daring to step out; he had bravely paved the way. This child had provided an exit, a way of escape for someone in my community. And now I had the notion that perhaps I, too, did not have to put up with this either and that, even though I had gone against my feelings about it before, what was happening in our house was not okay.

A long time after the incident with the broken table, there was one more life-changing event that sealed my fate.

I cannot remember what I was playing but I was in my bedroom.

My room was plain and tidy. Within its walls was a single bed, with pink bed sheets and bedspread which had plain pastel pink quilting and a flowing fluted valance. The bed head, which was also pink, was against the wall just underneath the window which overlooked the street. At the opposite end of the room was my Barbie house which

I had wanted for a while and finally managed to get as a Christmas gift. The wallpaper in my room was beautifully girly, just like a rose garden motif.

I also had a tiny radio which I kept on the windowsill. I would often play music which I had grown very fond of from Jazz FM, but on this day, I had not opted to play anything at all.

I was very used to entertaining myself, as Esther often called it, and I loved to host tea parties with Barbie, Cindy, Cabbage Patch and Teddy. Esther had gifted me with a beautiful china set of teacups and saucers and I would fill the teapot with water that magically became tea and serve my dolls and teddy.

I was very attached to my modest collection of dolls and had made a special and secret vow that I would never grow up and forget that they were real, unlike the rest of these silly grown-ups.

My bedroom door had been open; I was blissfully pottering around in my room. I heard the front door; my father came into the passage and stopped by my bedroom door. Esther quickly came to greet him where he stood, but there was something different in the air that afternoon. Something I could not adequately explain other than to say it was uncomfortable, just like when heat starts to prickle your skin.

There was an unfamiliar glare that my father gave me which instantly sent shock waves through my body and unsettled me. I was sure Esther felt it too, but she was not in charge of our home anymore; what my father said was law in our house.

I remember the room getting smaller around me and

my father telling Esther to close my bedroom door behind him as he walked into my room. I knew she was still on the other side of the door because I never heard her footsteps leave.

Something was very wrong. There was a strange, unfamiliar air about him. My heartbeat quickened for fear of the unknown that I could feel was coming my way. My mouth dried up.

He sat on my bed where I was also seated, facing me; he ordered me to open my mouth.

No. I internally cringed. But I had no voice. No power and no choice. As his face pressed against mine, I promised myself this would be the last time.

*

It's the morning of my fortieth birthday, a huge milestone to arrive at. This is the age that my Grandma Charlotte was when she breathed her last breath. I am grateful for life, health and motherhood.

Many of my past birthdays have been spent without family. Today is no different, however this time I am also without friends because of Covid-19 restrictions. But it is the sweetest feeling to know that this is my first birthday with you growing inside my inner space and the last birthday I will ever truly be alone in this cold world. I feel so attached to you that sometimes I worry about how I'll deal with you being outside of my body. But I can't wait to see you and for you to see me.

I recall fond memories of the life I have lived before you: fun parties, long lie-ins and beautiful holidays that I thoroughly enjoyed. But now, having done all the things I wanted to do, I am at a stage in my life where I am content just to look back at those well-lived times without missing them. It has been said that life begins at forty, and I am ready to begin a new life with you.

I wonder what life has in store for us. I know it will have its challenges, but as someone who had to grow up in an unstable family full of betrayal and heartbreak, I pray that your childhood bears no resemblance to mine and that I find peace of mind within myself.

As the day progresses, I potter about content in the fact that although today may not be filled with lavish celebrations, it is a day filled with gratitude.

Once upon a time, not so long ago, I became so withdrawn and depressed that I didn't want to exist anymore. The reason I chose to live in a big house in the middle of nowhere, deep within the tranquillity of the English countryside, was because of the depression I had suffered.

I craved the space and seclusion away from people and the busyness of London, to allow myself time to heal and rediscover whoever it was I was supposed to be.

This space, this home, has been the haven that allowed me to recharge. For now, you are making yourself at home inside my body, but soon, this house will be our first home together. A world of our own. Here, surrounded by so much nature, I have gained a fresh appreciation for life. I stop to smell the roses; I am alive to the intricacies of nature's garden.

I enjoy things again, all the small things that could be taken for granted, like dawn breaking and the morning call of the birds or the little deers that randomly wander into my back garden that I quietly marvel at. I am here, with you, on the edge of a dream that I thought had been shattered.

A flurry of unexpected birthday gifts arrives. I am so touched by this show of love, it warms me up on this cold spring day.

Sometimes it feels so easy to accept Esther's words – 'your best friend always has a better friend', she would often say. But these tangible gifts of love and remembrance of my birthday tell me that no matter what, I am loved. And if I could go back to tell little me anything, I would take her hand and say, "Please hold on; life will become worthwhile. You will be loved. I promise."

*

I had now started year seven of secondary school, which was very different to primary school. I loved school for so many reasons; I loved learning new things, but I also found the cultures and characters of the other children fascinating. Most of them seemed so confident and loud; I, in contrast, was a little mouse, quiet unless someone told a joke. Then, I would be the one laughing the loudest and the hardest. I found that laughing would mask my discomfort and soften the hard edges forming inside me. I know now that that laughter was simply a trauma response to the sadness surrounding my home life. Of course, I'd be cornered by the teacher for causing a disturbance, whilst everyone else who was responsible was able to fully compose themselves in a timely fashion.

My favourite class was humanities, but I was also fond of the teacher. So much so that in desperation to get some help to deal with the secrets within the walls of my home, in my head, I searched for ways to communicate this to her somehow. Something inside me had ignited; I decided to write Miss Susan a letter. She seemed like the perfect person to confide in as she seemed so caring and had this distinctive warmth about her. The lessons she taught us were about people and human interaction, so in my mind it made perfect sense to go to her because I felt she understood people better than anyone. Undeniably, it also helped that I could tell she was fond of me.

The letter I wrote outlined the abuse Esther and I both experienced at home. I could not have verbally voiced the secrets of my world outside school to anyone. I didn't quite know how to express it because there was a part of me that doubted I would be believed. But also, saying it out loud, though it sounds silly to say, made it even more real, and I didn't want to make it more real. It was already too real, I knew that, but vocalising it was just too overwhelming.

I always seem to lose my voice in confrontational situations; I just never know how best to express myself. I get all nervous, lose my chain of thought and feel very defeated before I even try to speak. So, for me, the best way to confidently express myself has always been to pen my thoughts.

Expressing myself in this way has been a haven, where no one can cut in and correct my feelings. But it has also provided the time that's often needed to absorb and work through them.

Dear Miss Susan,

I am really frightened and alone and I don't know what to do.

There are things which are happening in my home which I think ought not to be.

Many times, this scared girl is hit and mistreated by her father, and when her mother tries to jump in to prevent it, she is often beaten too. Once when I came out of hospital after an injury I had, my father stood on me to see if I would wince in pain, but this little girl was brave and held her breath and did not wince, for who knows what he would have done if she had shown weakness. I am not sure if he was impressed that she had shown strength in that moment or just amused, but he had this smirk on his face.

Miss, please can you help – I don't want to stay at my house any longer, but I really don't want to get them into any trouble.

Maria.

When I slid that letter under my teacher's door, unbeknown to me, she had been off school that same week. After a few days of nothing happening, I became very despondent, desperate to get help, but I guessed I would have no choice but to wait until Miss Susan came back and read my letter. Now that I had made that leap of faith, it was all I could think about. Though I was stuck in a type of limbo, there was no way of being able to move forward without a change occurring.

I kept imagining what would happen once she read the letter. Would I be helped or just told to stop making a fuss and get on with it? I would go through moments where I doubted I had done the right thing. What if all I had done was made the situation worse? I panicked about things getting even more out of hand.

Then there were other moments where I would daydream of a nice family waiting to embrace me, where I'd be happy and safe and loved beyond measure. I began to wish that the family I had been born into was not actually mine. And there had been a dreadful mistake of switched babies at birth. Surely my real parents were out there missing me, even if they had another child that had taken my place. Surely they would turn up one day, after years of searching for me, their lost child, and take me away from this hell. I could picture it all, those loving parents, turning up to claim me as their child. I saw a full, warm embrace with arms opened wide and warm forehead kisses filled with apologies for not finding me sooner. Their embrace would be a comfort and would signal to me that I was safe. No more missed meals because it couldn't be provided for, no more beatings or angry faces. And no more fear. But as much as I hoped and dreamed, I also felt guilty. Despite everything I had gone through, I felt that those feelings were betraying my parents. That perhaps I was a terrible child and maybe one who deserved to be punished.

I had started secondary school and had been given a bit of independence by way of taking the bus by myself to and from school on occasions.

On the not-so-odd occasion when Esther would decide to collect me, it filled me with dread. I was ashamed to be embarrassed of her. This embarrassment was not the usual dread and annoyance that most adolescents would feel towards their now uncool parents; instead, mine was from a place of knowing that if she was going through a season of relapse, she would have very public outbursts. "Your vaginas smell sour like fish," she screamed, loud enough for the whole school to hear. The girls would hold their stomachs and roar with laughter. That injection of acknowledgement had the effect of hyping Esther up, as though this was a paid audience that had come to see her. But this performance had me clutching my head in my hands, lying to myself that if I didn't look at the girls who were amused by Esther, then they wouldn't see me; they wouldn't notice that I was her child and that this woman was my mother.

What was taking the ground so long to swallow me up already? I kept willing it to, but it just didn't happen. Instead, the ground left me visible and exposed and extremely vulnerable to the teasing and whispers that would follow the next day at school.

"You must learn to wash your vagina, so it doesn't smell," they mocked. Hadn't I endured enough? Was this still going on? Surely God himself would take pity on me and scoop me out of this horrific scene. *God, please make it stop, pleeease!* I begged from the inner depths of my soul, but it was no use.

The last time Esther met me from school, I had made my way home and she met me at the bus stop as I was disembarking.

"Hello, chipmonk," she greeted. I hated being called that pet name.

"Hi, Mum," I replied. "Is he there?" I enquired.

"Is who there?" said Esther.

I was starting to lose patience with Esther; she knew good and well I wanted to know if my father was home.

"Is *he* home?" I pressed.

"Oh, don't worry yourself about that, come, come with me, walk with me and let's go to the doctor's surgery; I have an appointment," said Esther.

I loved Esther, but these days she was making it awfully testing. The more dismissive she was of me and what was happening in our home, the more I resented her.

As we walked the five-minute journey from the bus stop to our doctor's surgery, I knew that I could not go back home; I just could not take another day or another minute of *him*. If she was not going to protect me, I would have to stand up for myself. I did not know how; I had no master plan. All I knew was that there was absolutely no way I was prepared to deal with the situation anymore. Whatever the future had in store, it had to be better than this.

Esther greeted the receptionist; her name was taken, and she was politely told to take a seat and wait.

It had not been long since we had both been seated before her name was called.

"Do you want to come in with me?" Esther asked.

"No," I replied, shaking my head. No sooner had she disappeared out of sight, I walked calmly out of the doctor's surgery and ran as fast as I could. My heart was beating like a drum against my chest and my lungs were burning like a blazing fire. After about five minutes of running, I spotted a bus coming in the distance and jumped on it.

I had no plan and just the clothes on my back – my school uniform – but I resolved that I was never going back.

Within an hour of running away, I found myself at my best friend's house, 'Buju Banton'. She was obviously not Buju Banton the Jamaican reggae artist, but her Turkish name was close enough sounding to the artist and so some of the kids would reference her as such.

As I knocked on the door, I did not know what I was going to say to her. I had no idea about much else apart from the fact that I would never go back home again.

"Hello." It was not Buju; it was her older sister who answered the door.

"Hi, is your sister in please?" I asked.

"Beeeeeeeee, it's for you," she shouted out.

No sooner had B appeared at the door, all defences were down; I wept inconsolably.

What followed that evening was a series of statements taken from me at the police station.

"Why did he hit you?" a policeman asked.

"I don't know." I shrugged. I felt like a fraud even at the mere question being asked. This is not what people from my community did; you did not shop your parents, let alone speak family business outside of your home.

There have been many times in my life that I have been privy to kids jesting with each other about the varying degrees of discipline they received. I have spoken with adults who look back at getting 'beats' with a slipper or belt buckles for back-talking and such, almost nostalgically, as they laughed about it with their peers. So, what the hell was my problem, and why was I making such a meal of my experiences?

After statements had been taken, I was allocated an emergency social worker who introduced herself, then began hastily deciding where I would stay.

The sun had long since gone down, and it was pitch-black dark by the time the social worker and I arrived at a non-descript house and rang the doorbell. A woman opened the door and smiled.

"Hello," she said with a wide-open smile.

Oh no, I thought, as I noted she had a gold tooth. I'm not sure why this bothered me. Perhaps it's because I did not know anybody who had a gold tooth; nonetheless, it felt unfamiliar and unsettling.

In the morning I was ferried to a doctor for a physical examination. I was ushered behind a curtain in the doctor's office whilst the social worker waited on the other side. Once I had stripped down to my vest and knickers, I peered through the curtain, gesturing that I was ready. Both the doctor and social worker stepped inside the curtain where I stood. My entire body read like a map of scars. Every cut, every bruise and every scar was documented. That day was the end of one life and the beginning of another.

*

By the time my brother had been born, I was no longer living with Esther and had not been for months.

Esther had been moved out of her flat – by social services – to a completely different borough to safeguard me. All ties should have been cut between Esther and Joesph, but clearly that had proved unsuccessful because this new baby was born of both my parents.

Though I had contact with Esther and the baby, things were far from good between Esther and me.

Esther resented me for having made the choice to run away and whistle blow; she openly blamed me for my father's actions towards me.

"You must have done something to make him do what he did," she would jab. The more she jabbed over the subsequent years, the bigger the wedge grew between us.

I was determined to make my own way in the world as soon as possible; that's why I continued to work some job or another whilst I began studying for my A levels.

Having a job provided me with the resources to indulge in more quality fashion choices rather than 'The Black Market' (formally known as Lewisham market) range. I slowly began to take stock of the high street store fashions that caught my eye, such as Kookai and Benetton.

The thing that stood out to me, even at that time, was that although I enjoyed shopping using the fruits of my own labour, there were two things that weighed heavily on my back that gave me a sense of guilt.

The first was that, although I had money now, I felt I needed to consider whether that would be the case in ten or twenty years' time. What if by then I had fallen on harder times? So, with that in mind, during season sales I always made sure to buy items of clothing that were several sizes up in anticipation of the years ahead when I would be a proper adult. You see, I was no stranger to hard times, so whilst the going was good, I needed to stock up my storehouse.

The second weight was that every time I purchased something for myself, I had the overwhelming feeling that I should not just be spoiling myself but be thinking of the needs of both Esther and my baby brother. So, without fail, each time I purchased something for me, I had to ensure that I had the other two bases covered.

The biggest gesture I could make at the time was to offer Esther my first pay packet – the whole lot. It was important to me to help and make sure they were okay.

Once I finished my degree and managed to secure a full-time job in finance, I became even more disciplined. I worked hard to pay off all the student debts I had built up, then earnestly started saving.

My goal was to get onto the property ladder as quickly as possible and secure a real home for myself. You see, having experienced the instability of living in different people's homes over the years and even being told to leave with nowhere to go on my sixteenth birthday, the security of my own home meant everything to me.

The care system was harsh back then. If you did not have a good social worker who made sure you had some kind of social housing set up in time for the rite of passage into adulthood, you could quite easily find yourself homeless, as I did. So having a home of my own had been of the highest priority. Second to that had been the importance of ensuring that I maintained it so it would never be taken away.

By the time I was twenty-five, my hard work had paid off. I had done it; I had secured a mortgage on my own one-bedroom flat. Though I had reached my goal, I was not satisfied. That guilt that I explained earlier, it never left me. I had pangs of pain each time I thought about Esther struggling with my little brother.

Once I had pulled together a spreadsheet of my income and outgoings and knew exactly how much I had to play with each month, it was time to step up on my responsibilities to the family.

I could have easily given Esther money, but I did not trust that she had the ability to budget as well as I could. I decided the best course of action was to commit to buying her groceries each month and getting them delivered to her; at least that would help take the edge off.

The next thing I did a few years later was pay off all Esther's debt. Using some of my savings, I proceeded to wipe the debts on her credit cards and rent arrears away. Finally, I was able to exhale.

Even though I had managed to help in a few ways, I still always wished that I had been a little smarter and earnt substantially more. I recall watching one of the contestants on the TV show *Big Brother* mentioning that he had bought his mum a house outright – I only wished I could have done that for Esther. It would have fulfilled her dream of owning a house, but I could only do what I had already done. And in my mind's eye it was not enough. I had fallen short. On the inside, I kicked myself for it.

So, no, I did not want to have children because I already had two dependants and I did not want to add more to my load. I had felt like a mother to my mother, and a second mother to my brother, for the longest time.

As a young adult it seemed that all around me, people of my age were beginning to get into serious relationships and settle down. It was a normal question for people to ask if I wanted to have children, but I would often reply, "A child where?"

Three

When I grow up

I am changing your nappy, making sure to wipe all your crevasses clean with tender, loving care.

I am particular about the products I use for you; I want everything to be as natural and good for your sensitive skin as possible. I apply coconut oil to nourish and protect your skin before the next change; I'm lingering just that little bit longer, getting so lost in you while your skin breathes before being wrapped in a fresh nappy. Just as I am finishing up, I only have enough time to blink, before I am suddenly covered in a warm, mustard-coloured mush.

Ohhhhhh, I've been hit by a 'poo-nami'! I am stood frozen in disbelief. How can someone so small and so adorable be capable of this offence? Honestly, I don't know whether to laugh or cry. I'm sending out an SOS; what on earth am I supposed to do first? Should I clean you up for the second time, or should I lay you down somewhere safe so I can get myself washed up?

How, how did I get here?

I remember planning out my hopes and dreams for the future with my friends back at school. I thought I'd be married with kids by twenty-five. Now here I am, a forty-year-old, single mother to my beautiful baby, aka, my little poo machine.

*

"When I grow up, I want to get married and have two children, a girl and a boy."

"How old do you think you'll be?"

"Definitely twenty-five."

"Yeah, me too."

"Me three!"

Throughout our time at secondary school, Tameka, Hope and I were like the three musketeers.

Hope was of Nigerian heritage and lived with her mum and younger brother in Deptford.

Tameka had become my bestie, though I think she was still warming to me. She lived with both her parents and quite a few siblings at home. Both her parents were Jamaican and lived in Forest Hill.

Then there was me, predominately raised by a single mother but now in care. As I clung to my mother's heritage, I was also the unpopular 'small island' girl, now residing near Lower Sydenham in London.

Our commonality was not just the colour of our skin, but it was the fact that we shared hopes, dreams and aspirations. We wanted to succeed in life and hoped to obtain more than our parents.

We would often walk home from school together even

though we lived in opposite directions from each other. The point of our walks was so important to us – we wanted that time to express our hopes and dreams and talk about how we envisioned our lives would be when we got older.

It felt empowering to vocalise those dreams. I hoped that the universe was listening and would treat us kindly.

I was fourteen when I realised I had a crush on my first black boy. He was different from my usual type – not just in skin tone – he was tall and slender (for the longest time I had deliberately avoided boys who resembled my father in any way). The one thing that differed from my father in his appearance was that he was dark skinned. And one difference was a win enough for me, plus he was cute and looked like Busta Rhymes.

This boy – Matteo – seemed to be quite the joker. He was very loud and confident when busting jokes at the back of the 122 bus.

As it transpired, I was not Matteo's usual type either. I was way too geeky, uncool and a nobody in school to ever be paired with such a popular boy like him. Hell, I had not even peaked yet.

Let me be frank, I was ugly and Essie has pretty much co-signed this but stating that "you're not pretty but just attractive". If I pulled my 'fro all the way back, I could have quite easily passed for a boy. The only thing that set me apart were my hips and bum.

Matteo's type was quite specific. He had a thing for Jamaican girls with big breasts, broad hips, thick thighs and bum. Mostly girls at school who had their hair permed straight and their edges slicked down with gel in a wave-like pattern down the sides of their face. Accessories were also a must-have statement. These 'cool' girls wore gold not silver; they wore these big hooped earrings and at least a gold chain or two that would dangle proudly around their necks like medals, at least until they arrived at the school gates and would have to tuck them inside their jumpers. The finishing touch was a sovereign ring and being into dancehall and ragga music, which I absolutely hated with a passion. I did not understand any of the songs and it made me feel very uncomfortable.

Though I was black, most, if not all, of the other black girls at school did not see me as one of them. In fairness I was completely different in the way I spoke and my geekiness. The only way they could make sense of me was by labelling me as a 'bounty': black on the outside and white on the inside. Perhaps they had a point; in fairness I could not relate to them or the music. I did not even have rhythm unless I was given choreography by my dance teacher in class.

I was very much in touch with my version of Afro-Caribbean culture, but I had not been exposed to this type of blackness at such concentrated levels, and it showed.

I don't recall the fine details of how it came to be that Matteo and I got together. What I know is that I had mentioned that I thought he was cute to a girl from school as we sat on the bus approaching the local Boys' school on-route to our stop at our Girls school.

Her boyfriend happened to be a friend of Matteo's and, of course, he was also jesting and wilding out at the back of the bus with the other popular boys.

The girl called out to him as I cringed with embarrassment. There was no way his friend Matteo would look twice at me; the news of this preposterous overstep was going to get me beat down and laughed at in school.

There were further whispers between Matteo and his friend, which was awkward as hell. This would have been a good time for the floor to swallow me up. You have got to be kidding me. I heard their footsteps, then saw them both coming over to where I sat. They towered over me; it felt as if I was being inspected like a bird in a cage.

Matteo smiled at me and gestured at my school friend to give up her seat beside me so he could sit down.

Now it was just the two of us. Me and this cute boy in this two-person seat at the back of the bus. Meanwhile, everyone else's voices seemed to fade away into the distance as if no one else was even there.

We soon arrived at his stop outside the boys' school, but we had already arranged a double date by then. How on earth did I manage that? Everything was a haze.

Matteo and I dated from the age of fourteen right up until I was eighteen. He and his family knew all about me being in care, but unlike most people during that time, they were completely unphased. I found them to be most welcoming and soon became a full-fledged member of the family.

I genuinely got on with all his family; in fact, I probably dated them as much as I was dating Matteo. His mother would refer to me as her daughter-in-law, and his nephew Jack, who was in our age group, became one of my closest friends.

We were inseparable, Matteo and I, he just understood me to my core, especially when I messed up. And boy did I mess up a few times.

I would do silly things to try and test him, or get him to prove his love, but subconsciously I was sabotaging the relationship.

Thankfully he was like a Jedi – the force was with him. He had this far-reaching understanding of me that I didn't even have of myself at that time. He had this uncanny ability to understand the root of my pain and why I was lashing out in the way that I did.

He gave me a pass during my many moments that were fuelled by fear or anger and pain. So, I chose not to abuse his gift of grace; instead I vowed to myself that I would do better. And I did. I never repeated the same mistakes twice with him because I loved him. And by his actions and not just his words, I knew without a shadow of a doubt that he loved me too.

Over the years together we would talk about the future and what we wanted from life. Even before he had said it, I already knew he wanted to get married and have a family. But he also knew that as much as I admired him for that, this desire of his was not my immediate goal.

I wanted to go on to university and try and make something of myself. It was so important to me because I wanted to be the exception to the rule. I was determined not to be a statistic or any stereotyped connotation that were part and parcel of being a child of the state.

I knew some of the girls who I had gone to school with quickly became young mothers and it really did not appeal to me at all. I did not want to have a child and struggle; though I knew Matteo and his family would support me, I needed more.

Perhaps it was this mindset that made us break up in

the end, but I was determined to set up a proper future for myself.

Matteo had always said I was clever, so it should not have come as a surprise to him that I chose to explore what I could become and what I could make of myself over a life of forever with him.

They say that you can make plans but sometimes life has a funny way of showing you and your plans who is really in charge.

Tameka and I had decided to meet in Peckham and have a little shopping spree in Primark; way before Primark was even popular it had always been good for the odd top. You could never go wrong with some pyjamas and tights.

We had not been shopping that long when I started to feel funny. I felt so hot and sweaty, it was as though I was losing control of my body – I was faint. Thankfully Tameka was there to prop me up, but I had never felt like that before.

"Let's go and get some Mackie Ds," Tameka suggested.

I could barely respond because I felt so faint and so unlike myself. We slowly walked up the high street to the familiar golden arches of McDonald's. I was beginning to fear that I would lose my balance.

Tameka was a stand-up girl. She was level-headed, smart and had great foresight. But for her to show concern meant it was pretty darn serious because not much moved her.

As we ordered our meals, I had a light bulb moment and quickly decided that I needed to add extra gherkin to my order. That was strange as I had never done that before, but as we sat down and began eating, I started to feel better.

"Tam, can I have your gherkin?" I asked.

A few weeks later when my period hadn't shown up, it was clear what my body had tried to tell me before. Sure enough, I was pregnant. And Matteo, of course, was the father.

"What do you want to do?" Matteo asked.

"Well, there's no way we can keep it; I mean, where would we live, what about uni?" I reasoned.

"We'd figure it out, Princess, I don't want you to get rid of it; I know it's your body and, ultimately, it's up to you, but you know I want us to settle down anyway; it just makes sense we…" Matteo cajoled.

"We are in no position to be parents. Do you really want to be like every other statistic out there struggling to make ends meet? I can't live like that; I'm sorry, I just can't," I concluded.

"I'll support you no matter what you decide; you know that," said Matteo.

Two weeks later I had a termination. I decided on going into hospital for them to put me to sleep. When I came to on the ward, I saw another girl I knew just across from me. Clearly, we had both chosen the same option but neither of us wanted to acknowledge the other. It was too deep, too private and way too personal for anyone outside of those closest to us to know what we had done. So, no words were spoken, no further eye contact made. Zero judgement was the agreement we silently made.

Matteo and his older sister came to collect me from

the hospital so I could be discharged; we drove back to his home. I had already squared it with my foster carer the week before that I would be staying at his for a week or so just to cover my bases.

As I lay in bed that night with Matteo snuggled next to me, I was thankful that he had my back.

What I did not realise at the time was that my decision broke his heart. Naively I had underestimated just how much Matteo wanted that baby. I also failed to realise in that moment just how much he hated me for having a termination.

*

I'm curled up on the floor weeping uncontrollably. I'm sure I've already cried a river, but the tears keep streaming down my face.

Even though I have changed your nappy, cradled you, sung to you and done everything else I can think of, you have been crying relentlessly for hours. Nothing seems to be working and I feel helpless.

The sleep deprivation is killing me. I have been running on empty, catering to your needs and feeding you on demand every two hours. Now I am at my wits' end, unable to comfort you or myself. And just like a baby often does, I cry myself into a welcomed sleep.

Four

Sitting with fear and regret

It's cold outside and the rain is falling down; you are asleep as we lay skin to skin in the warmth of my double bed. I am so bewitched by you my eyes can barely take you in.

A few weeks ago, when I turned forty, you were still inside my womb. Now, your 'new baby scent' tickles my nose and fills up my senses – I think I'm addicted; I wish I could bottle it forever. It has been said that 'good things come to those who pray', well, you are certainly a good thing.

*

Esther was a woman of faith. Having come from a family of churchgoers, she raised me just the same.

Every Sunday she made sure my clothes were pressed and we went to church. I enjoyed Sunday school.

We attended an Anglican church called St Silas which we would walk to from our home.

The church was nice enough; though the numbers in its congregation dwindled, its members were committed.

Even without seeing the high and perfectly constructed ceilings and beautifully stained-glass windows, a blind man would know he was in a church building because of the distinctive scent of incense.

As the thurible swung along the aisle of the church, the incense and our prayers floated up beyond the edge of the sky.

The day I stated to Esther that I wished to be confirmed, she was thrilled. I felt ready to confirm the promise she had made to God during the dedication ceremony in my infancy.

"Oh, Chipmonk, God will bless you!" said Esther.

She could not wait to overindulge in the preparation of buying a white confirmation dress, veil and white gloves.

Before I could be confirmed I had to attend Confirmation classes, which not only encouraged you to grow in faith but taught you about the creed of the church and explained the meaning behind certain practices.

Now, I was sincere about the faith aspect, but I also wanted to be able to participate in all aspects of the service like the other church members. Honestly, I had a keen eye on the Holy Communion wine. Back then you got *real* wine in a goblet. I still giggle about that. The only downside for me was having to drink out of the same goblet as everybody else.

Later, during my teenage years, I left the Anglican church. A girl from my secondary school invited me to her church; I was open to the prospect of another denomination. As far as I was concerned, although other churches had their own way of doing things, if they were worshipping Jesus, the saviour of the world then that was fine with me.

Nothing could have prepared me for the experience of a Pentecostal church.

As soon as you walked into the church, the music and vibrant energy hit you in the chest. There was a full band playing drums, keyboard and guitar. The choir that accompanied them were so gifted with their harmonising, they could have won the TV talent show *The X Factor*.

The congregation had their spirits lifted higher and higher, until they were up on their feet one-two-stepping, clapping or raising their palms to the sky in sweet surrender. It was quite something.

I had never been to a predominantly black church before; it was quite an adjustment for me coming from the Anglican church which was predominantly white. The other major adjustment was the dress code. First, the women's hair looked salon fresh. Not a hair out of place. And either make-up was immaculate, or fresh faces looked quenched as they glowed.

The men wore suits, like those you might expect to see on 'city slickers' with high-end jobs. The women never wore trousers. They wore skirts or dresses that didn't rise above the knee even when seated. I struggled with that aspect of the dress code. My past traumas meant that wearing a skirt made me feel unsafe, vulnerable and violated.

I could not even wear a nightdress to bed; it always had to be pyjamas. Trousers were an important defence and protective for me. An unholy war began raging on and on inside. But of course, I never confessed this. So, nobody knew it but me.

There also did not seem to be anything fashionable that I felt comfortable in as a teenager that was also appropriate for church. It was the nineties; I would like to have considered myself a fashionista. Every morning before college, I would watch 'Vital Statistics' hosted by Johnny Vaughan and Denise Van Outen on *The Big Breakfast* show. Whatever Denise was wearing on the show inspired my outfit for the day.

Despite the dress code conflict that I had with this church, its practices intrigued me, so I attended for years.

The young ones who attended the church struggled to maintain the lifestyle that was expected. Expectations were high as we had all been 'saved'; going to parties or having boyfriends was frowned upon.

We straddled the lines between commitment to faith and our adolescent desires. As we battled our way through the minefield of this grey area, it became apparent that I had not yet figured out who I was or where I fitted.

Every time I went out with friends who were free of any convictions of faith, I had pangs of fear that at any moment God would strike me down. Though I loved God and everything that church offered, there was still a longing to be with my old friends and not have the weight of guilt interrupt moments where I just wanted to have fun.

This constant battle within me was a killer of old friendships and a killer of the life Christian faith required. I often found myself in a state of purgatory over popular forms of adolescent expression.

In the end, long before my teenage pregnancy

occurred, I decided that the lifestyle church required me to lead was not sustainable. So, in a bid to be honest with myself and God, I decided that I could no longer practice as a Christian, but my faith remained intact.

As a pregnant teenager, I had serious doubts that I had the capacity or the means to provide adequately for a child. I wanted far better for my child than the cards I had been dealt.

When I decided to terminate my pregnancy, though I understood it was a sin in Christian terms, I felt it was the right thing for me. Nonetheless, I made a vow to never get myself into a situation like that again.

There have been moments when I have wondered what mine and Matteo's child would have been like. I could never quite picture his or her face, but I'm sure he or she would have been beautiful. I wonder how I would have managed as a young mum. Would I have resented missing out on opportunities to travel or develop a career? Would becoming a teenage mum have changed me for the better or worse? Maybe I would have soared and never looked back. Maybe.

When I reflect on the darkness surrounding my decision to terminate that pregnancy, I am confronted by a sea of emotions that leave me gasping for breath. Now, over twenty years later, armed with full comprehension of what takes place when you have an abortion, I fully regret taking that life. I do not think that writing those words or saying them out loud will ever express how deeply disappointed and regretful I am with my decision.

Nobody ever speaks of or informs you of what happens in surgery when you terminate. Admittedly, I didn't seek out that information either; I think in the moment, there is a part of you that would rather not know.

It took many years for me to finally pluck up the courage to read up about the procedure in detail. I was horrified by what I read. Furthermore, I came across ongoing, yet disturbing, research that contradicted the established view that the foetus feels no pain. That knowledge broke me. How devastating to know that at my request, my foetus may have felt the pain of being snatched from the place that should have been the safest in the world.

The surgery takes less than thirty minutes. And while the mother feels no pain as she lies seemingly lifeless under anaesthesia, she is oblivious to the experience that the tiny life forming inside her is about to have. When you wake up to your new reality, full of guilt and sadness, you wonder why people would ever believe in happy endings.

I will never use my faith to demonise the choice to have an abortion. It is far too complex and sensitive a decision for anyone to make; women should be supported through it – not condemned. Some people may say that perhaps I think that way because I have partaken in the act; I can't argue that there is not an element of truth in that.

What I do know is that God gives everyone free will. It is up to you and I to choose which paths to take, then commit to developing the capacity to bear the weight that surely follows.

My choice has stayed with me; for every passing year, I continue to wonder and grieve. In my lowest moments, I ask myself, *am I any different to somebody who has chosen to take a life in some other way?* Though other people may not see the blood on my hands, I do. They may not see the images that sometimes flash before me of a life that I caused not to be here, but I do. They may not hear heartbeats fading into nothingness, but I do.

I often judge myself just that little bit harder, or hold disappointment in myself just that little bit longer, because I blame myself for the choices I made in my past.

My issue with abortion is more of a personal issue with myself. I find it easier to extend grace to others than I do to myself. I have learnt a hard lesson about choices you make and can never take back. Those choices stay with you underneath it all and you may spend a lifetime trying to make peace with them. But never again would I break the sixth commandment: thou shalt not kill.

*

A diamond undergoes the highest degree of pressure to be formed. It's been years of longing; it has taken my whole life thus far and everything I've got to form you. You have had to survive the untold pressure of turmoil in my inner space to be here now in my arms. I am not sure I deserve this priceless moment, but I know that you deserve to be here.

You stir slightly, then nuzzle further into me; I hold you closer than close as my neurons light up. I finally get it. So, this *is true love.*

Five

Punching above my weight

You are taking your first steps, a couple of staggering motions at a time before you fall into a sitting position. I watch on close by; I'm cheering you on with pride and willing myself to give you the space to learn. You get up on your feet to try again and again as I stay ready to scoop you up should you need me.

It's so amazing to witness your steady progress and development in these first few months of your life. I smile at you and hope you know that I would gladly go to the edge of the universe to catch you every time you fall. My life-long pursuit of happiness is over; I'm happy that I am willing and able to protect you as any mother should. I think when you were born my heart instantly grew and my arms became wings. These precious moments are not lost on me; they make me consider my own childhood and the evolving grief I still feel for the mother and daughter relationship that never was. We all grow up, but do we ever grow out of the desire to be mothered? Sometimes, I still long for someone to catch me when I fall.

I am aware that I'm flawed, but my love for you is flawless. You continue to stagger around. For a moment I think ahead and imagine a time when you are much older and still need me, one way or another – I will always be here to break your fall.

*

There is an elite section of black men who have always seemed out of reach. Let me qualify that sentence. There is an elite section of black men who have always seemed out of reach to *black* women.

These men tend to work in the city, are doing exceptionally well in their careers, earning a six-figure salary long before they even hit their forties. These 'city slickers' not only have money and brains but are also still down to earth and, invariably, proud of their humble beginnings. Now, those guys are my idea of the perfect eligible bachelor.

I met Jeff and his friend William by chance; I say by chance because, though I was the lone, black female 'slicker' – by the way, scarcity in the workspace was the main rationale offered by Jeff for why black men like him were rarely partnered with black women; I suspect it's a little deeper, but that's for some other book to delve into – working for the same company, in the same multi-floor office building as them, we first met and got acquainted in a drinking hole a stone's throw from our building.

Jeff was a lovely, down-to-earth guy who had done well for himself; once I got to know him more and we became friends, I was even more impressed. He was in his thirties and had almost finished paying off his mortgage; he was a saver but by no means tight with his money.

He had not gone to university; he had got an apprenticeship, then built up years of experience and landed a role as a vice president within the financial world.

He could cook well; his culinary skills displayed how knowledgeable and worldly he was. He was as real as they come. I could talk to him about real life experiences, and he got it. Good chat, good banter. That was Jeff.

Jeff introduced me to his friend William who, in contrast, had this sternness about him. I felt uncomfortable and insecure around him. William was tall – perhaps the personal, negative connotations I held about height was what made me feel intimidated.

Whenever I was in William's presence, I could feel myself trying to overcompensate. I would be jovial in an over-the-top way, and he would snap.

"Why do you always have to crack jokes, can't you ever just be serious?" he would say. His comment was a kick in the gut. I felt foolish for trying too hard but didn't know how else to be around him. His tone reminded me of my father. I did not like it one bit. He made me feel like an absolute numpty!

I wondered how William and Jeff were even friends. On paper it made sense: both high achievers who had grown up together. But to me, they seemed so different in character that I struggled to see how their friendship thrived.

Nevertheless, I hoped to find myself someone of their calibre, despite worrying they were out of my league.

Throughout the years, we developed a bond, and I felt more optimistic that I would meet someone like them – a perfect match of my own.

When Jeff transferred from our London office to Asia, it forced William and I to try and get on a little better.

We were never as close as Jeff and I had been, but we had a reasonably good friendship. When we finished work at the same time, we caught the same train, then he would offer me a lift the rest of the way home. Once in a blue moon, he would call me at the weekend saying he was round the corner from my flat and ask if it was okay to pop in. Sometimes, he would be renovating a house he had bought and would invite me to come and see it to share my thoughts.

I saw William as such a catch – he was attractive, but I was not attracted to him. Had our personalities married better, that could have been a game changer, but even after all this time, I still found him a bit prickly.

Have you ever felt that you were punching above your weight, then, having got with the person, wondered why you had placed them on a pedestal? Well, fast forward, I had changed jobs and now worked in a different financial district.

It had been a few years since I had caught up with William, so I decided to reach out and organise a catch-up. He obliged and we met after work for a bite to eat.

Something had obviously changed in me; I no longer seemed bothered by William's sternness. Perhaps I had just accepted that was a part of who he was, or maybe he had learnt to soften his approach towards me. Finally, we were meeting each other in the middle.

As if by magic, our communication flourished; we went from old friends to lovers.

William's perspective was that we would simply be able to navigate into a different type of relationship because we had known each other for years, whereas I was of the mind that I really did not know him, so we needed to start from square one.

It wasn't long before I started showing signs of struggling to adjust with him. It had been a while since I had been in a relationship. I was not used to sharing my past with just anyone; I had become quite guarded.

Unfortunately for me, William was straight in like a dog with a bone. He was unphased at whether I was comfortable with his line of questions; he just wanted to know the answers.

"I've never heard you talk about your family, tell me about your parents?" he quizzed.

I thought to myself, *please just back off*, though I would never have said that out loud. Instead, I took a deep breath and held onto it for longer than I should have.

"Ermmm, my mum, urmmm… lives just up the road from you, actually, urmmm… she used to look after kids but she's retired now and, ummm… yeah," I fumbled.

"What about your dad?" William pressed.

"Oh, he was a bit of a rolling stone, so, umm they aren't together. I don't really see him," I offered, reluctantly.

"What about your brothers, how many do you have again and what do they do for work?" William enquired.

Gosh, it felt like twenty questions. I was not coping well under the pressure of his questions at all. What might seem simple and innocent things to ask someone you have just entered a relationship with, were constant reminders of how fragmented my version of family was.

Having been in care I had no one, not really. Yes, I still had contact with Esther, but it had been a long time since I had seen her as a mother, and my baby brother could have been my son.

My kid brother and I did not have much of a relationship; any effort trying to forge one was hard work. My fear was that perhaps he had lived with Essie too long and her illness had rubbed off on him. It is so easy to become a product of your environment; they were both so co-dependant on each other, and It was all too much for me.

Since I had made the decision to stay in care, all my friends from school had grown to accept my new family as my own: the lady with the gold teeth, I now called Mum; her three sons, I called my brothers.

This same lady had obviously grown on me; after a few years of living with them, I wanted to be an official part of the family. I wished she would adopt me.

I would dream that she had decided to adopt me, then imagined her hosting a welcome party for me, with all the family.

*

I'm lying awake in bed in the middle of the day, daydreaming away. And as I settle into what I wish could be my reality, I feel my body relax and my heart fill with love as images of an idyllic fantasy float into my head.

I see myself in a scene that I have created a thousand times, my version of a happy family: arm in arm with my new mum and my brothers surrounding me in celebration. Their warm glances assure me that I am now a part of something special: a unit, a family of my very own. And I have never felt as welcomed and loved or a part of something as I do in this moment.

A piece of paper is presented to me – it's official – my new mum has adopted me. I have proof that I am theirs and they are my new family. For the first time I feel worthy of love. I have arrived at the finish line of one life filled with pain and disappointment, but this line also marks the beginning of my new life, in a loving family that I have craved forever.

The feeling of love and acceptance is the most incredible energy I have known. Finally, the family-shaped hole inside of me has been filled.

*

When people asked about my family, I would refer to my new family. But there would be times when information I gave was not consistent because I was caught between two places, or should I say, two families. I had always clung to Esther's heritage, but my new mum was from a different Caribbean island, so sometimes I might say I was one instead of the other which would throw people off who knew my brothers.

In many cases where people knew the boys, they would always comment and say they did not know they had a sister. And I would stand there feeling a heatwave of embarrassment.

William was genuinely asking about family out of interest. But his interest was going to put me in that dreaded position of having to bare my soul, then feel the judgement and pity of the person listening. Perhaps, that is why I had not got into many relationships. I hated the F word: foster care. It was as offensive to me as the crudest swear word. The association brought judgement from many.

I had worked so hard to separate myself from it, but it followed me around, just lingering in the air. Irrespective of my many accomplishments, I would always be seen as a foster child. That killed me a thousand times over. It is my perpetual torment, my Achilles heel.

William looked at me with this piercing look; he knew there was something I was not telling him.

"Babe, how are we supposed to go deeper if you keep holding things back?" he asked.

He was right, but as right as that was, I was not yet ready to unveil my story. I needed time, patience and trust. None of which he was giving me the room to feel. He just kept applying the pressure to give up that which I held closely locked away in my soul.

A week later, after much rehearsing in the mirror, trimming down my story to give enough without giving him everything, I told him.

His response was so nonchalant it offended me. He had no idea what it had taken for me to say those things out loud. He had got what he wanted; to him the exchange was successful.

I resented him for it. For making me delve into the darkest parts of me sooner than I had been ready to; I felt violated all over again.

Despite how I felt on the inside, for William it meant

we could move forward in our relationship and start making plans.

I guess the bright side of sharing showed me that William did not judge me negatively for any of it, which under normal circumstances would have been refreshing. However, the timing of it to me had been so premature that in many ways it had put me on the back foot.

The strongest component that helped us to regroup was that we both wanted the same things out of life.

I was now in my thirties and William would be knocking on fifty's door soon.

Though he had a child from a previous relationship, who he adored, he was eager to start a family. And for the first time in my life, I felt like I wanted to have a child; I was ready.

It had been many years since my abortion; I felt, at least financially, secure enough to shoulder the responsibility of a child. I had always told myself that should I ever become pregnant again, I would keep the baby without question.

Here we both were, William and I, discussing having a family. He had already given me keys to his place; it was all moving positively in a direction we both wanted.

But of course, life being life, there was a possible spanner in the works. My fibroids.

I was in my twenties when I discovered something was wrong. I had been lying on my bed, just listening to some music, and by chance I happened to brush my hands over my lower stomach, in a bid to ease the tightness of my skinny jeans from around my hips, but in doing so I felt this large mass protruding from my otherwise flat tummy.

My doctor felt it too; he referred me to a gynaecologist. When my appointment came through, I met with the specialist who explained that the mass was large: a whole 6cm for my small 8–10 frame.

The specialist did not feel there should be a course of action at that time, according to him – aside from the heavy periods they caused that would cause me to flood through my clothing in seconds – they were not causing me any problems.

However, I was concerned about them disrupting my future family plans. As common as fibroids are, particularly amongst black women, there are things to note that can signal bigger problems on the horizon, such as their position, how many and the size.

I questioned them on whether this would prevent me from having a family in the future. The response was a roundabout way of saying – possibly.

Funnily enough, I discovered I had fibroids back when William and I were just friends. Will had taken time off work to support me at one of those appointments.

Each time I would ask about the potential bearing this would have on my fertility, each appointment I left with a little less hope than the last.

Just before Will and I started dating, my cousin Kate and I had discussed our fertility. The life of female 'city slickers' meant that starting a family was put on the back burner; it was not unusual to consider freezing your eggs.

Kate and I decided to attend an open day at a fertility clinic to investigate our options.

Now that Will and I were together, making plans, I

was not as geared towards freezing my eggs. But I thought it made sense (given my history) to at least have some fertility tests carried out to check my general health so we could get cracking. I asked Will whether he would consider getting checked too.

"I think I want to have some tests done, you know, just to check I'm all good, and they'll probably be able to tell me how many eggs I've got. I was kinda thinking it makes sense for you to send off a specimen," I said.

"Huh, specimen for what?" William asked, horrified.

"Look, we're making plans for our future – we're in this together – it makes sense we both check we're good, right?" I reasoned.

"Nahh I dunno about that; I don't think I need to, I mean, I've got a son, I've clearly not got any problems on my side, and there's never been any problems in my family," he retorted.

"I hear what you're saying, but you had a son ten years ago; you're a lot older now," I said.

"How much is it?" William said.

"About £150," I said.

"How much! Uhmmm, I don't know, let me think about it," William exclaimed.

And with that, the case was closed.

Though we were still together, I knew William did not feel comfortable at the prospect someone might question his manhood, so I left it and proceeded to have my own tests done.

Kate and I went together to the London Women's Clinic on Harley Street.

We had already attended an open day about a month

before which informed us of the different types of fertility that they dealt with and processes of each.

Harley Street clinics are known for being the best of the best; we were happy to go ahead and have our examinations and tests carried out.

The doctor I saw asked about my medical history and whether there was a particular reason I had come to have these tests carried out. I explained my concerns regarding my multiple fibroids.

I let him know that I had not officially started trying to conceive but had hopes for the near future. I enquired whether I would have the option of being able to freeze my eggs to alleviate any undue immediate pressure.

After our conversation, I was directed out of the consultation room and into an examination room.

There, I was met by a female nurse who got me to undress my bottom half and sit on the bed and cover myself with a sheet.

With both the nurse and doctor present, I was given an abdominal and pelvic check; the doctor confirmed that he could feel my large fibroids. Next came a transvaginal ultrasound; I hated anything intrusive and found it uncomfortable. There was a television screen on so I could also view the inner parts of me, but quite honestly, nothing could have distracted me from the discomfort I was feeling.

"I can't quite find your uterus," the doctor said as he gestured for me to slide my bottom further down the end of the bed.

"That's better, now just cough a couple of times for me please, yes okay, we've got it," said the doctor.

My uterus had clearly decided that now was a good

time to appear for inspection, but I understood why she was hiding – what could be more mortifying than all your dignity being thrown out the window?

I got the feeling from the glances the nurse and doctor gave each other that I was unlikely to pass this exam with flying colours, so I braced myself. My moto had become, 'prepare for the worst and hope for the best'. But as much as I tried to cling to hope, I had this sinking feeling that the results were not going to be favourable.

"Okay you can get dressed now; the nurse will come back in afterwards," said the doctor. As soon as I was alone, I sat up and wiped the gel away from around my vagina with the paper sheet I had used to somewhat conceal my body. I slipped back into my knickers and jeans and sighed with relief; it felt good to be back inside the safety of my clothes.

Now it was time for the bloods to be taken.

These blood samples were going to test for my FSH, LH, Oestradiol (ovarian hormones), Prolactin, my AMH (ovarian reserve), day twenty-one progesterone test (ovarian test) and a test for thyroid function.

The wait for all the results seemed quite long. I could not help but worry about the possible implications of my large fibroids.

After an age of waiting, I was welcomed back into the consultation room with the doctor. Suddenly, the room seemed dark and uninviting.

I sat in the chair opposite the doctor; when his lips began to move and he began to speak, my heart began to sink. The hopes I had for a family slipped further out of my grasp with each word he spoke.

The doctor explained that the internal exam had shown I had two large fibroids, which was of no surprise, but the glances I had picked up on during the examination now told their story. My left ovary had no antral follicles. A healthy number of follicles would have been eleven to twenty; I had zero. Although my right ovary had some present, it was not enough, and the quality was poor. My cavity had also been affected by the size of the large fibroids.

My bloods had come back with equally unsatisfying news. They pronounced that my Mullerian hormone levels were at the lowest end of the spectrum. This spectrum was between 1.1 and 53.5 for my age range, and the closer to 53.5 the better; my hormone level was at 1.3.

I could tell the gynaecologist was doing his utmost to deliver the results as sensitively as possible, but it was clear that he did not want to give me false hope.

He stressed that I had a low chance of successful conception, naturally or with fertility treatment with such a low AMH.

It was suggested that my situation needed further investigation and that I should have an MRI to locate the exact number of fibroids to confirm possible damage to the cavity. Should the cavity be affected as he predicted, fibroid surgery might improve access to the left ovary, however, there were no guarantees that access to the ovaries would mean they would respond to ovarian medication during ovarian stimulation.

Again, he pointed out that this was due to the low AMH level and the fact no antral follicles were present on the right ovary.

The realistic chances of success using my own eggs were so bad, he suggested that I would be better off not wasting my time, but instead, I should try with a donor egg.

As this information poured out, all the facts and findings, all I heard was, *you can try, but honestly, it's unlikely you'll be able to have children.* My fate was sealed.

I would not be able to conceive naturally. I did not even have the option of freezing my eggs because of their dire state.

The advice given to me was that my best and only option would be IVF. I had very few follicles in my right ovary and of diminished condition.

For me to improve my chances of IVF it was strongly suggested that I have the fibroids removed as soon as possible. The removal would firstly create the space for a life form, which I did not currently have, but would also help to lessen the chances of miscarriage.

My hormone levels indicated that I was premenopausal. This began to make sense of why my periods were so irregular. In recent times, I had started going months without even having a period.

I felt like my head was going to explode.

All my hopes and dreams for a family were obliterated.

At the end of the consultation, I walked slowly down the winding staircase, back to the waiting area where Kate was.

"Are you okay, cuz? You look…" asked Kate.

"No, and not today, I just can't," I replied, despondently.

We headed back to the underground in silence. The rest of our journey was much the same. We embraced before going our separate ways.

"Babe, how did it go?" William enquired later that evening when he called.

"Not good, I'll speak to you properly when I see you at the weekend," I said. That night, I went to bed with shattered dreams.

I needed at least the week to process this catalogue of heart punches. I wondered how William would take the news, but this wasn't even about him; it was about me. Right now, I needed to find a way to cope with feeling like less of a woman; I needed to find a way to cope with feeling deflated about *everything*. I could not achieve the thing that came so naturally to millions.

Now, I was fully aware that God was not at fault here, and that this was all on me - a sure consequence of my own actions, but how typical in this very moment for a little devil to sit on my shoulder, and dig its far-reaching fork into the tenderness of my soul reminding me that this was my punishment for breaking the sixth commandment? I kicked myself inside and rolled my eyes in dismay and disappointment.

As I gazed out of the window of my room, the devastation of my circumstances flooded back again. Looking out at the open field and rolling hills beyond, I abandoned my body and slowly drifted. I disappeared further than the landscape my eyes could reach, and wondered whether I had made the right decision all those years ago; ending my pregnancy and leaving Matteo to go to uni – just to end up here. I was alone and full of longing for the life that being with him would have given me: a home, love and a family.

I was haunted by the choices of yesteryear, with far fewer options than I could have hoped for or foreseen.

If life is a game of chess, then I missed the rule book, and now I, the queen, was left vulnerable, exposed and unprotected.

No matter where you stand in life, there are times where the grass always seems greener. We reason with ourselves as to why, without question, our ambitions navigate us to those greener pastures, but what if we've got it all wrong, and it's all just a game, testing you to see what it is you hold dear?

William and I sat down over the weekend and went through everything the doctor had relayed.

"Look, I don't believe what they've told you about your fertility, I mean you still have your periods, so that means you have eggs. But I do think you should get the fibroids removed before we start trying properly," he said.

But as the following weeks rolled by, I felt an increasing distance between us. I did not feel he could comprehend my pain and suffering, and I felt he was perhaps ill equipped to comfort me. He already had a child, any more would be a bonus for him. But for me, having a child was now the most important objective that I was unlikely to reach.

We often go through life on autopilot, but there are moments that are so fraught, they force us to pause for breath to re-evaluate everything all at once.

Subconsciously, everything I had done up to this point in my life was in preparation for a family. I was not a millionaire by far but had secured myself financially to be able to provide for a family one day. I bought jewellery that could be passed on as heirlooms; I made sure I had enough savings so that should I decide to stay home for a few years as a full-time parent, I could do so without putting financial pressure on my partner to carry us all.

After all the years of professing to not wanting a child, the tables had turned and shattered. My life now resembled those tiny fragments of glass from Esther's table that my father had sent crashing to the ground all those years ago.

My life felt like a constant fight for survival, my efforts to not sink but swim were being tested. I was weary. It felt like I was going under, and nothing would be okay ever again.

My feeling that William could not just be there for me told me that it was time to get off the ride and figure out my next steps alone.

I knew for sure that I could no longer provide him or myself with the future we had planned and hoped for. William never said that he had doubts about our future, but things began to feel different between us since my situation came to light. To me it seemed as if deep down he was struggling to communicate that without me being able to have a child, there was no future for us.

The break-up was inevitable. One evening, I let myself into William's house where he lay sleeping in bed. I packed up all my clothes and things into a bag I had brought with me. I left his house keys on the side table and left. It was over.

Time was not on my side. Emotionally, I felt I could only do this now while I had the strength to go it alone – yes, I had decided to go hurling towards the possibilities of IVF by myself.

I knew my chances were slim to none, but I had to try. Otherwise, regret would pull me down all over again.

I was about to enter the ring in the fight of my life. And my opponent was Mother Nature.

I knew that, emotionally, I would only have the capacity to deal with one round of IVF. I was clear that one try was my lot. The procedures I had been through so far, I found heavy. I knew that stepping into a perpetual cycle of trying and retrying would be the undoing of me.

I carried out enough research to understand what I would need to do. Going for IVF and needing an egg donor as well as a sperm donor would send anyone, let alone a single person, into a financial bind. But can you put a price on life? Can you put a price on hopes and dreams? By my logic, if people were willing to spend thousands of pounds investing in their education by way of university, then why wouldn't I apply that same intentness to my plight?

My mind wondered back to William. Had I done the right thing in leaving him? I had to reason that if he was lacklustre about going for a fertility test, it was questionable how supportive he would be towards IVF.

Still, I could not shrug off how daunting it felt to be considering going through IVF alone. Naturally, I feared the unknown twists and turns. Though I was sure I would not be the first or the last single woman to put herself forward, I questioned if I was the right single woman to do it.

Would I have enough mental strength to see the process through and deal with every eventuality? This was about the creation of life and the rebirth of me as a lone parent. I felt I had no room for error. As imperfect as I was, I felt the need to be perfect. The pressure was enormous.

My head was bubbling with thoughts and questions,

doubts and concerns, I needed to get this junk the hell out of my head before I spontaneously combusted.

I had talked myself out onto a ledge but was now feeling so unsure. I was about to admit to myself that perhaps I was biting off more than I could chew, when it dawned on me that my foster brother Adrian had had serious issues with his fertility a few years back. I needed to speak to him straight away.

I called Adrian and explained my situation and the undertaking that I was considering on my own. Immediately, he was so compassionate and told me he would support me every step of the way. "Sis, you don't have to ask; I know what you're going through; I'm here for you. Any appointments, consultations from here on, I'll attend with you. You don't have to do this alone," he said. Without hesitation, he was right by my side.

Adrian was such a kind-hearted person, he just had this spirit that brought joy into the room. You did not have to know him well, he only had to be in your midst to have you smiling or laughing.

I was so touched by his offer to stand by my side, I knew that he meant it wholeheartedly. His was the kind of support that gave me the freedom to feel everything that was burning inside my chest: the maternal, the rage, the devastation, the hope. There's a comfortable silence that you can have with someone who understands your plight in a way no one else can because they have been through it and come out on the other side. Though doctors had pronounced him infertile, he had gone on to have two beautiful boys, naturally. He understood my tears as I cried down the phone. In those shared moments, I knew I would no longer have to bear this alone.

Adrian was my foster brother, but we had never lived together. He had been fostered by the same family as me; when I had been placed there, he had already been living independently for a few years but was still a huge part of the family.

I don't think either of us knew back then just how bonded we were as siblings, but now, we had two commonalities that only we knew and understood. We had both been in care, and we had both been diagnosed with infertility. I honestly believe he felt my pain; it was an unwelcomed pain that he knew only too well.

I wasted no time making an appointment with my GP; I explained the findings and advice from the private medical tests and consultations.

I had researched hospitals with the best track record of success in IVF. I felt confident about the hospital I decided on, so, when the GP asked me where I would like to have my myomectomy, I stated my first choice with my whole chest. Choosing the right hospital at this stage would ensure an smoother transition to IVF.

I was referred to my chosen hospital and soon met with the assigned consultant. Once again, I went through my medical history, the tests at Harley Street and their findings.

My new consultant felt it best I undergo the tests again with him, just to double-check everything.

There was one test, however, that he advised I have, which I had not had before. This was called a hysterosalpingogram (HSG) test. This test would determine whether my fallopian tubes were blocked, especially given the size of my large fibroids.

I am still scarred by the experience of that test. I remember the day clearly. I had been nervous, because this test was more invasive than anything I had ever had before.

All the research about the procedure assured its reader that you might feel a little discomfort but nothing more, but honestly, I called tomfoolery.

I do not do pain well. I am the girl who takes two doses of paracetamol before a bikini wax. So, it was standard procedure to prepare myself for this in the same way.

Upon arrival, I was told I needed to take off all my clothes in a cubical and put on a hospital gown. All jewellery had to be removed too. Once I was ready, I was called into a large room that looked like an operating theatre, all stainless steel and soulless. In the far corner I could see the radiologist in a booth. As I adjusted my gown and got onto the examination table, I was so scared I had to hold back a flood of tears.

It was not hard for anyone to see my concern; I must have looked like a rabbit caught in the headlights.

A kind nurse present in the room stood by my side of the table and tried to distract me by first holding my hand, then asking me general questions about hobbies and things of that nature.

This attempt to distract me was not working, I could feel everything. I felt the cold instrument of the speculum enter my vagina, and then as though being wound up like a clock, the gynaecologist then proceeded to tighten the speculum in a bid to open my vaginal canal wider and wider.

My cervix was then cleaned with some clear fluid and then in went the cannula. Injected through the cannula was a dye that would be visible on the x-ray, if there was anything blocking my tubes, it would be visible.

As the dye began to flow through the tubes of the cannula, I thought to myself, *it is not that bad*. But I had spoken too soon. Within a few seconds, I started to feel this enormous pressure building up within me; the pressure quickly turned to discomfort, then excruciating pain. Never in my life have I felt anything like it. To me it felt like I was being tortured. How could this be happening in 2019? It felt barbaric.

I was at the point of no longer being able to withhold floods of tears. I tried to stay composed for a few more seconds, but I could not bear the pain.

"Please stop!" I cried.

"Do you want to end this procedure all together?" the gynaecologist asked.

"No, no," I said. "I just need to pause for a second, then you can continue. How much longer do you think this will take?" I asked.

"I cannot determine that; I just need to continue," they stated, matter-of-factly.

"Okay, I'm ready," I lied.

More dye was injected, and the pain got worse.

"Sorry, please stop," I pleaded.

I was so embarrassed that I was not managing this better, I could feel the mounting frustration of the gynaecologist.

"Do you want me to end the procedure?" they asked again.

"No, no, sorry I just needed to pause again," I kidded myself.

One last time, we tried again. This time, I could no longer fight the pain or be brave like the many women who had done this before me. I had reached my pain threshold moments before now; enough was enough.

"Sorry, please stop – I can't do this anymore. Do you think you've got enough?" I asked, hoping.

"We won't know right now. Do you want to end the procedure?" they asked.

"Yes," I sobbed.

I continued to sob as I slid off the table once the instruments and tubes had been removed; I sobbed as I put my clothes back on.

I was completely inconsolable, not that anyone had tried. I cried and cried for the trauma of the invasive procedure I had just had but also for the trauma of what was to come by way of IVF. As I left the hospital, I became that person that you may have seen once walking down the street, in floods of tears.

A few weeks later, I received a letter confirming the results.

MRI multiple large fibroids, the biggest around 10cm and the second one around 5cm. One ovary seems to have been pushed high up on top of the uterus and will not be accessible vaginally. Hysterosalpingogram shows that the uterine cavity is okay; one fallopian tube is not patent.

Overall, the prognosis was extremely poor for trying to conceive naturally. And very poor with IVF, using my own eggs.

Two months later, a few days after my thirty-ninth birthday, I was back in another hospital gown. The day of my myomectomy had arrived.

I had been scheduled for surgery early in the morning; my older cousin Trigger, whom I hadn't told much about what was going on, accompanied me. I was directed into a room to get changed; afterwards, I returned to the waiting room where Trigger sat with my suitcase and other belongings.

A doctor entered dressed in scrubs; he confirmed my name and date of birth, then confirmed that I would be having an operation to remove my large fibroids, which if for any reason went wrong, could result in a hysterectomy.

"I'll come back when we're ready for you," he said, before leaving the room.

Soon enough, the doctor returned; I walked down a short corridor with Trigger and the doctor in my gown and a pair of long white compression socks. Trigger then waved goodbye and took the escalator to exit the hospital. I continued with the doctor down the hall and into the pre-surgical room.

In the pre-surgical room there were two medics, a female anaesthesiologist and a male surgeon. I was directed to sit on the end of the bed with my back facing them.

First, a section of my back was cleaned with what felt like a wet wipe, then a needle – filled with local anaesthetic – was injected to numb my back. The sensation was so weird. Instantly, my back felt desperately itchy, as though insects were crawling all over it. Then, I had to lean forwards, making the frame of my back concave. Most importantly, I had to keep as still as possible whilst the epidural needle was inserted.

"Owwww!" I winced.

"What can you feel?" the medics asked.

"I can feel the needle on my right side," I replied.

"What about now?" they enquired.

"Now it's moved to the left side," I said.

It was not painful, more a shock and slight discomfort. As soon as I had alerted them to what I could feel, the impact lessened.

They quickly finished and I was asked to lie down on the bed on my back and count backwards from ten. I don't believe I got any further than nine before I was out for the count.

A few hours later, I was wheeled into recovery. I was groggy; my vision was blurry. I was awake but not fully present. A few moments later, I was crying and screaming in agony. A medic tried to calm me down and quickly administered more drugs.

I could have sworn that the surgeon came by to tell me the surgery had been a success and that I would need three months' recovery before they could start IVF. Everything was such a haze.

Once I was back on the ward, everything seemed fine. I was comfortable at least. All things considered, I had been very lucky to have had that operation. At the time, a new deadly wave of Coronavirus – Covid-19 – was sweeping across the world and moving closer to Britain. There were constant talks of a national lockdown being imposed.

It wasn't just my own world that was turning upside down.

Like the rest of Britain, I had of course heard the news weeks before announcing how rapidly the virus was spreading. But naively, I thought things like that wouldn't hit dear old 'Blighty'. But I was wrong.

I stayed in hospital for three days, during which time I appreciated the support of friends and work colleagues who visited me before I was discharged.

Among those visitors, my foster brother Paul and his long-term girlfriend Lisa. Paul was not a foster child; it was his mother – the lady with the gold tooth – and his family who had fostered me.

Paul was our mum's middle child. Growing up together, our relationship went through ups and downs, but at this point in our lives, I felt closest to Paul out of the three boys. In many ways, this was surprising because Paul had always been the cool guy who everyone knew, and I had never been the cool girl.

Women loved him; they found him terribly attractive, which they often attributed to him looking like LL Cool J. Paul was not modest – he knew he was good looking. And he had the gift of the gab. Paul wasn't just popular; he seemed to know the crème de la crème of ex-footballers, football agents and coaches and other socialites. A world I clearly did not fit into.

I did not have the right look to be in and amongst the 'populars'. I did not wear much in the way of designer labels or have 'good hair'. I didn't know any celebrities or have his type of contacts.

I loved Paul, but I always thought of him as quite superficial. Not only that, but in the back of my mind, I thought that he would choose his friends over me any day of the week. It was a weird thing to think, but soon, I would be proven right.

Lisa suggested I come and stay with them while I recovered; I appreciated her support. I was in a terrible state and had picked up a nasty chesty cough. Now, under normal circumstances that would not have been a problem, but I had just had abdominal surgery – each time I coughed, I had to grab a pillow and grip it tightly around my abs so that my stitches wouldn't burst. It was so painful. I became so aware of how much you use your abdominal muscles for everything.

I could barely walk; I moved at the pace of an OAP with a Zimmer frame. Sitting down on a chair or, worse still, the toilet, had to be done slowly.

Paul collected me from the hospital; I had to be wheeled to the entrance then helped into the back seat of the car by Paul and a porter. It was a long drive back to south-east London from south-west London. The closer we got to their house the more humps there seemed to be in the road. Each hump we went over was excruciating. I would yelp in pain. I just wanted to cry.

I stayed with them for three weeks. I was unusually high maintenance given the circumstances that recovery demanded. I was unlucky enough to pick up a reoccurring infection, just to add insult to injury.

Paul had to take me to the local hospital near their house to get treatment several times and get my stitches checked. My stitches stressed me out. I had been advised how crucial it was that they be taken out at just the right time. Too soon and I imagined all my giblets would fall out. Too late and my skin would bind itself together with the stiches. They were not like having a cross stitch or something to that effect; they were a combination of internal and external stiches that were held in place by two metal bands on either end. It freaked me all the way out.

When the day came to finally have them removed, one end had to be cut and then you had to slowly pull this string like cord for a length of at least 8cm. None of the nurses were familiar with the stitches I had; you could tell they were nervous about getting it wrong. I feared I might pass out, so the nurses offered some gas and air. Yeah, the stuff they usually offer to women in the throes of labour; the irony was not lost on me. After a few inhales of that stuff, I felt a little less scared and a tiny bit tipsy – the way I would after a shot of rum and coke. There is nothing worse than needing to have a procedure done and not having full confidence in those around you to carry it out. I felt so scared and vulnerable; it was not a nice position to be in. Thankfully, the nurses managed to do it painlessly in the end. I thanked God that was over with.

I had been staying at Paul and Lisa's for a while and was very conscious of how well they were looking after me, but I did not want to overstay my welcome. Esther had been my example of repaying people with kindness; I could hear her saying that people's memories were often short. It was important to give back so that no one could ever reproach you. I made sure to order takeaway for us every Friday. It made me feel a little more comfortable knowing that, in some way, I had contributed.

They had been kind enough to let me stay, but the fact that I was not blood related weighed on me. Deep down it was my feeling that sometimes people can have a little less patience and understanding in such cases; I felt like

I was becoming a burden. I did not want to feel that way, but I did.

The day I left their house, Britain went into lockdown. It was something that none of us were completely prepared for or had experienced before. It was such a strange time. Governments had no real control over this virus, but they certainly exercised their power over the people. The impact of the virus was life-changing for millions. The losses were devastating. The NHS, though crumbling under the landslide, was heroic. I was in no condition to do much of anything. I was fortunate to have some friends make the couple of hours' drive up to me (I had moved out of London and was living in the East of England at that time) once or twice to drop by with food and other bits to keep me going, which was a complete godsend.

My recovery was coming along slowly. After a few more weeks, I was able to walk up a flight of stairs, happy days, but I still needed crutches to aid my mobility.

Trying to lift my leg over a bath to attempt having a shower was a complete no-no, so a wash in the sink with a flannel was as much as I could do.

I appreciate my solitude in the best of times, but in the worst – when you're desperately trying to recover – it can feel like the loneliest kind of lonely. I'm sure that going back home, where I lived alone and nobody lived nearby for support, had set my recovery back. But somewhere deep inside I could hear Esther's mantra, 'don't beg, don't borrow and don't steal', sounding like an alarm on repeat. So, somehow, I dug deep to weather the storm; I guess I *can* stand the rain. But the truth is, what other options did I have?

Six

Seasons change

I wake up in a panic fighting for air. Now sat upright in bed, I am working hard to steady my breaths; I'm gripping the moist sheets around me for comfort. As my breathing regulates, I slowly exhale and take in the room around me. I am not at home; I am at rehab. It's okay; I'm safe; it was just a bad dream.

Though I can rationalise that I have woken from a nightmare I have no recollection of, I am left with the distinct feeling that something very real has happened to me, at some time or another.

I can feel a prickling soreness around the lips of my vagina; it burns at my touch; it feels so tender as though it has been bruised. I wince. I don't understand what's going on. It's just me here alone in this room; the chair is still against the door in the same position I had left it.

An hour later I sit in my group therapy session. I have been inconsolable since my dark nightmare; the therapist asks the rest of the group to leave the room.

"What I want you to understand is, sometimes, when something too traumatic has happened to us, the brain tries to protect us by burying that traumatic event. Though it seemed real, what you are feeling is not something that has happened today; it is something that could have occurred somewhere in your past.

"These sessions are very intensive; it often causes the things that have been buried for so long to resurface.

"You need to accept the horrible things that happened to you in your past to allow yourself to heal. You are healing, and with healing comes strength. It wasn't your fault. None of it was your fault," the therapist consoles.

It is the first time this has ever been said to me. I begin to digest her words and, for the first time, I fully acknowledge that the things that happened to me in my past were not my fault.

*

Time can often heal many things. Accordingly, after three months of recovering, I began to get back to normal. Britain had moved out of the strict lockdown, though we were effectively in a lesser lockdown state with people being encouraged to stick within their support bubbles. The world had changed and continued to morph into this 'new normal' state of learning to live with Covid-19.

As I scrolled through my phone's memory of names and email addresses, one name – Brian – stood out as if it were blinking at me like the cursor on my laptop, calling me to action. Brian was an old flame. For reasons that will become painfully apparent by the end of this chapter, answering that call to action is the moment that I changed the course of my life.

Now, let me tell you, our story. I was in my twenties when Brian and I first met at a music awards show. He had won an award that night.

I had been dining on one of the round tables close by with my bestie Jack, completely oblivious of Brian or his group.

Jack and I had planned that whole weekend. We stayed in an apartment a stone's throw from the venue where the awards were taking place, all so we could crawl back from the after-party. Our outfits had been prepped for weeks, if not longer, we both looked every bit the part as we walked the red carpet.

My 'fag hag' years were amazing. Jack and I always had such fun getting into good trouble together. Everything was always 'exclusive'; that was our word for everything fabulous. More often than not, we had good trouble on our minds, and we knew how to have a bloody good time.

We had just bumped into his cousin who was a well-known artist. After a few minutes of exchange, I excused myself to go and powder my nose. As I entered the toilets, a guy walked past; I quickly realised it was unisex.

In typical female fashion, after I had finished the necessaries, I took my time in the mirror reapplying lip gloss. I was almost finished when this strapping guy walked through the door.

I was such a sucker for a good navy suit and crisp white shirt, my jaw must have obviously dropped to the floor because he looked at me, smiled and casually said, "So do you."

Damn! How on earth did he know what I was thinking? Oh, yeah, jaw – floor.

I have never attributed beauty to a guy before, but to me, he was beyond gorgeous – he was beautiful.

Something told me to hang in there, not to leave. So, whilst he went in one of the cubicles, I decided to stall by the sink mirror to see if we would strike up some conversation once he came out. Minutes later, he was washing his hands at the sink next to mine; we got talking. He introduced himself as Brian; he said he was there with his brother and some other people. I mentioned I was with Jack. We exchanged numbers, then went back to our respective tables.

There were several after-parties that night; I think Jack and I went to most of them. At one party, the VIP area had been sectioned off upstairs on a balcony inside the club, which overlooked everyone on the dance floor below. I left Jack to go upstairs where there was a masseur with an empty table. I could not believe my luck – I jumped at the chance of a massage. From there, we went onto the Hilton, then another venue, then another. Before long it was 5am. The birds were in full voice doing their morning call when we crawled back to the apartment. My feet had a grievance with me for wearing heels to party into the early hours. We were young, reckless and fun. What a night.

Later that morning, just as we were packing and getting ready to leave, my phone rang.

"Babe, who's that ringing your phone at this time of the morning?" Jack enquired.

"Babe, I have no idea – I don't even recognise the number," I replied.

"Well, you better answer it then, babe," said Jack.

"Hello, who…?" I started.

"Babe, who is it?" Jack bellowed, even though he was right next to me lounging on the bed as I sat down.

"Oh, my gosh, Brian, hi!" I exclaimed.

I could not believe it. Beautiful Brian had called me. He wasn't doing the playing it cool thing of waiting three days; he was straight in. I loved it.

He casually mentioned that he had only been at the awards last night because his band had been told they were going to win. Now they were at the airport flying somewhere, but he said we should meet up when he got back.

I finished the call. Jack was waving his hands at me in his typically flamboyant fashion. He commented that Brian must really like me if he called straight away.

I was chuffed, not because he turned out to be one of the artists who had collected an award that night, but simply because he just seemed so lovely and down to earth. Many guys would have delayed calling to save face, so I found it attractive that he had the confidence to go against the grain and go with what he wanted to do regardless.

A week later, Brian and I met up. It turned out that he was also from South London and only lived up the road from me.

Our first date was at a restaurant in Blackheath. As we sat there getting to know each other, we discovered that we knew some of the same people. He knew two of my mum's sons as they had gone to the same secondary school together.

He probed as to how I knew them and what the connection was. I tried to leave the F word out of it and just said that their mum had looked after me when I was younger.

But he was not letting me get away with that; he wanted to know exactly what I meant, but I was not about to reveal the skeletons of my past on the first date. It was way too soon for all that; things were going so well that I just wanted to enjoy the moment. I managed to dodge his line of questioning, at least until another time.

It was a lovely sunny day, so once we finished eating, we made our way out onto the Heath and just sat down on the grass gazing at each other. Brian wrapped me up in his arms. He nuzzled his face into the side of my mine and commented that my cheeks smelt nice. His comment made me smile; he was so silly and quirky – I liked that about him.

There was something about Brian I am not sure my words can do justice. I found him captivating. Whenever we were together, whether at one of his gigs or just taking a stroll somewhere, it didn't matter who was around, I was completely lost in him and he was in me.

After a few beautiful months with Brian, I started to consider how we were going to work long term. I worked a nine to five so to speak, but in reality, my hours were much longer than that in the high-powered city. Brian's artistry started in the evenings, so it was challenging to keep a balance between the two.

We didn't break up in so many words, rather, we just fizzled out. However, the spark between us was never lost. Every now and then throughout the years we would catch up or randomly bump into each other and…

I guess our story could have ended there, the rest remaining unwritten after that ellipsis. But, well, it's a thin line between love and misadventure. It had been about two years since I last saw Brian, when I tripped and fell down that nostalgia rabbit hole by scrolling through my phone *that* day. Though it had been a while, it in no way felt amiss to email him for his support regarding a petition I was trying to put together.

We went from an email exchange, to a text, then a call. And before long, we catapulted into us spending time with each other at our respective houses.

It was so natural with Brian; things just flowed. Like a sponge, I couldn't help but absorb everything about him. It felt good; it felt better than good.

When we had dated before, we were so young and had so much room for independent growth. So much to learn and do outside of each other. Now twelve years on, it seemed we were both in a much better space with more clarity than before. He now had his own place, which made him more settled. He had also become a father. Although he was no longer in the relationship that produced his two children, fatherhood added another feather to his bow, because he seemed more loving and compassionate.

Before now I had not been as open to the thought of us in a real way, but now it felt different; it felt as though the stars were aligning for us to really be something.

The energy from our spark had remained intact for all these years. Moreover, we just seemed to have a lot in common that I had not realised before, such as being foodies, lovers of sushi and organic things.

Unlike those years before when Brian had tried to probe me about my background and connection to Paul and his family, I was comfortable with him and more assured in who I was. I knew my early childhood and adolescent past were not something I should be ashamed of. I no longer needed to carry the weight of my parents' mistakes; their shortcomings were not mine.

Brian agreed that had I been open about my past back then he probably would have judged me. But now he had seen a lot more of life, he had a better understanding. For the first time in a long time, I felt at peace and free with a guy.

We were back in our universe, all the stars and him and I. But there was just one problem: I did not know how to tell him about the choice I had made to go forward and try for IVF.

Before we got intimate again, we took the responsible approach to openly discuss the status of our health. This was new for us; in the past we had been more carefree.

This time we took measures to assure each other we were all good, so we were comfortable making love without any protection. It was not until a few weeks after we had begun being intimate that Brian asked whether I was on any contraception. I told him I could not have children so didn't need to be on anything. That seemed to satisfy him, so we left it at that.

Brian stated that he was not a fan of using protection, which shocked me because he also emphasised that he didn't want any accidents since he already had two young children. I found his stance mind-boggling. I had no problem with using it and told him that I was happy for him to use some. However, he seemed taken aback by this and firmly stated that he would not be using any protection.

The more time that we spent with each other, the more we were open about things that had occurred in our lives. Whether it was the fact of me being bullied at school for being different, or the fact that he had lived with a few girlfriends but never considered marriage.

I told him about the myomectomy, about how I had struggled with the recovery; he seemed sympathetic, which was touching.

Brian stated that ever since he had known me, I had never come across as the maternal type. To his credit, he had read me right all those years ago. But no sooner had that comment been made, it triggered a memory of us way back when we had been together – out of the blue, he had said that we should have kids. At that time in my life, that was not the place I was in. I had just arrived in a position where I was able to really help and make a difference in Esther and my brother's lives, so a child, or talk of one, certainly was not on the cards. The thought sent shock waves through me the moment he said it.

What the hell was he talking about – was he mad? I could have bitten his head off and spat it out in that moment. But instead, I composed myself and quizzed him on where we would live. His response could not have frustrated me more. He was so nonchalant that things would work themselves out. "Oh, we'd work it out," he said.

Suddenly he seemed less attractive. Now looking back, I can see that that was perhaps the catalyst in the demise of our relationship.

While on this memory train, I tried to refresh Brian's memory of all that. Unsurprisingly, he did not recall referring to us having a family but conceded that was very much something he would have said metaphorically. *Yeah, right!* I thought to myself. No wonder they say men are from Mars and women are from Venus.

At the start of mine and Brian's rekindling, I had told both Paul and Lisa about us. I didn't want to make a big deal of it, but on some level, it was more out of respect for Paul, given he was really close with Brian's brother, and they had just entered into a business partnership together. Had the families not been known to each other, my preference would have been to keep my affairs close to my chest, as I had always done. But as it stood, I didn't want Paul to hear it from someone else.

Paul let me know that he appreciated it. He went on to say that if he heard anything pertinent, he would tell me. I was rarely surprised by Paul but was shocked to hear that, in his opinion, Brian was good for me. To his mind, I needed someone who could dedicate themselves to me, which he felt Brian could.

I had never known Paul to give a compliment without some backhanded remark, so I braced myself for him to throw some shade. In his opinion, Brian always seemed to be absent from most of the family events that Paul had been invited to.

Okay? And? I am not sure what he wanted me to do with that information. Was that his cryptic way of warning me to just have fun but not to pin any long-term family-type expectations on this thing with Brian? Or perhaps, he felt his apparent lacklustre with his family meant he would inject all his time and energy into me? I didn't know, so I just shrugged my shoulders and brushed it off.

Whatever the point was, in my mind Paul, Lisa and I had become closer, which I appreciated. I would not usually have divulged things of such a personal nature, but our closeness had intensified since they had looked after me so well post-surgery. As we were talking so frankly, I disarmed myself and told them how close Brian and I had become; neither of them were shy about asking intimate questions.

Lisa remarked that it was a good thing that I had told Brian I could not have children and that I was not on any contraception. Apparently, in doing so I had covered myself should anything go wrong. She felt if those things were left unsaid, situations could go sour quickly. I appreciated her take on things; it made me more relaxed. I began to feel that perhaps I had said all I had needed to Brian. Maybe I could just exhale and not feel bad about telling him about my hopes for IVF. I resolved that certainly, for now, in this early stage of our rekindling, it was not necessary to mention.

In her efforts to lighten the mood, Lisa joked, "You need to get out there – maybe having a young guy like Brian is what you need to help things along, if you know what I mean," she said with a wink.

She's probably right, I thought. For the first time in what felt like the longest time, I was actually happy in a relationship. I saw huge potential for our future. But I knew I was the type to fall hard and fast, so I was depending on time to help Brian catch up with his feelings to see that we had something worth investing in.

Paul and Lisa both knew that I was seeing Brian; our communication intensified. They would text me when they knew I was with Brian, asking how things were going, expecting a blow by blow while I was in his company. It was too much. It was way too intrusive for my liking, family or otherwise. So, I respectfully asked that they step back and allow me to live my adult life without enquiries or interjections. They obliged and backed off.

Spending time with Brian was seamless. If I was at his house during the week, I would be logged on for work carrying out daily tasks and requests; he would be in the next room composing music or at the studio rehearsing. We coordinated our time well, took note where each other were going and when the other was back.

Whether we were together or apart, our thing had become watching *Married at First Sight* – it was our fun go-to talking point. For me, it was also a way of being able to talk about our own relationship to gage how things were going. Each week, the couples on this reality show discussed with counsellors how their relationship was going and decided whether to stay with each other for another week. Brian and I did the same, minus the counsellors.

Things felt so good with Brian. I felt it was significant to note at our age. We were approaching forty, both aware that dating can be harder when you're older because you're likely to be stuck in your ways. But for us, it was so far, so good. The one drawback that kept niggling at me was that I still had not told him that I was planning to try IVF. Not telling him made me feel dishonest.

I was in such a conundrum because I wanted to be open with him, but we had only just begun and I couldn't risk spoiling something so beautiful. No matter how good we were, this 'secret' kept pricking my conscience like a pine needle trapped between the threads of my clothing.

I was torn. The whole thing was beginning to affect my emotions. I was stressing out. I was in limbo, thinking, *should I, or shouldn't I?*

Adrian had this notion that I should tell Brian because he would likely want to help me through it, but I could not see that being the outcome. Through my lens, that scenario was unlikely, not because I saw Brian as uncompassionate, but because I knew he had his limits.

I asked a few girlfriends and my cousin Samantha for advice. Most of them believed it was too early to bring up the IVF, especially as I was not at a stage of receiving treatment. But the consensus was, once I began treatment, which included medicine I needed to inject myself with, it would be time to tell him and risk that being the end of us.

The hospital called – they advised that my payment had been confirmed, so it was time for me to start choosing a sperm donor so that it could be ethically transported to the hospital and stored, ready for me.

I had a provisional donor on standby whom I had met by way of an app called 'Just a Baby'. This guy had a great profile; he was clear about the process and had an excellent success rate at helping others create their families. I felt confident that he was a good donor choice – I liked the idea that, though he would have no involvement bringing up the child, he was open to meeting with the child should they wish to, at the appropriate time.

It was becoming real faster than I was now ready for, given my new relationship development. I had not bargained on the curveball of falling in love. Now the emotions of wanting a child and not wanting to lose the love I had found were colliding like rogue planets. I feared losing Brian but also feared making the wrong decision and losing perhaps my only chance to have a family on my terms.

My head was spinning. The emotional roller coaster was beginning to wear me down. How could I possibly choose between one love and another? Was one love more valid because it was already physically tangible over that which was based on blind faith? Was I just kidding myself on both counts? In the cold light of day, neither one of these loves were concretely mine.

I had only confided in two of my closest friends about my decision around the donor. Tatiana was completely anti the whole thing, which made me feel wrong for even considering such an option. The negative view that she held on this topic was so strong and piercing. I understood her opinions and the place that it was coming from; they came from a place of religious faith. Tatiana didn't believe that I should be going down this road of medical interventions to have a child; instead, it was her belief as a Christian that I should be praying and preparing as I waited for God to move my situation forward. I felt so disheartened. All I needed was for her to understand and empathise with my situation.

Despite our differences of opinions, that didn't change the love and respect I had for her. Only a true friend could be that brutally honest, though it was hard to appreciate in the moment, I knew that was why our friendship worked well. We didn't tell each other what we wanted to hear but what was necessary.

As I licked my wounds, I searched for a gentler response. I called my friend Cece. She was another good girlfriend; she knew me well and understood me probably better than I understood myself. She, too, was a woman of faith, but she had graduated in psychology, so her understanding of the human mind and human behaviour was her area of expertise.

She also had the ability to be very direct with her thoughts and views – she knew how to read a room well but communicate with a degree of sensitivity, which was more than welcomed.

I was still surprised how understanding she was about my situation and my IVF plans. She was completely empathic and open to medical assistance should one need it.

Her view was that you go to a doctor if you are sick, so if your womb is sick, why would you not do the same?

The lady from the hospital was still on the other end of the phone, advising me about the process of my donor egg transfer. It began to panic me. I hated being poked and prodded more than most – this was yet another essentially 'painless' but invasive procedure that would take approximately fifteen minutes.

After the last procedure I had at the hospital, which was horrific for me, I couldn't help but dread others that would follow. The thought of all these procedures weighed heavy on me, clothing me in a state of fear and trepidation. For this reason, I wanted to know everything in detail; I left nothing to chance and researched all parts of the process to mentally prepare myself.

However, when I stumbled on an actual video of the process in action online, it looked horrendous. Although it was under local anaesthetic, I still felt there must be a chance of being able to feel everything. With that in mind, I politely let the lady know that I was not interested in having the donor egg transfer carried out unless they put me under general anaesthesia. But we were still in a pandemic, which meant the theatres for general were not in operation and she did not know when that might change. So, I would be on the list and contacted as soon as they were back in action.

Relief flushed over me. This was great, I thought, as my IVF would now be on hold, it would give me more time to develop things with Brian before I had to tell him. I wanted nothing more than to enjoy this moment with him.

As the weeks flew past, I started to feel differently – I was compelled to challenge my perspective on everything I had been so sure about. It was mind-boggling; I had been so certain that I wanted to go through with IVF, but now, the fact that Brian and I had rekindled a relationship made me question if what I had wanted in having a family was the right path for me. Was there another, better, path that, until now, had not presented itself to me?

I had someone who I loved – perhaps if he felt the same way about me and could see a future, he could be enough. Loving him might be enough to fill the void of wanting a baby on my terms. He already had two children, so maybe I was destined to be a stepmother to fulfil my maternal yearning.

The problem was I was scared to tell Brian how I felt about him. In my mind I had figured he was not quite ready to hear it. And there were a few things that my friends had questioned about him and his sincerity that unsettled me.

He was lovely with me, and we were both extremely affectionate towards each other; I think it often surprised him just how compatible we were in that way. He cooked a lot for me, always making sure that whenever I was at his, everything that I liked to eat and drink was already there. But there would be other times, when we had not seen each other for a week, when he did not seem to miss me. That felt like a knife to the heart.

He would casually remark, 'didn't I just see you the other day?' whenever I asked if he had missed me, which bruised my confidence with him.

There would be other times when I felt he was inconsiderate of my time; he would make plans without giving any thought to me at all. It was as though I didn't matter or was not a significant enough part of his life to communicate with. I could be staying at his house and then at a moment's notice he would just spring it on me the night before that his kids were coming over the next day. It would enrage me, not because it was his turn to have his children, but for the mere fact that he had not considered me enough to give any heads-up, so I would be hurried to make myself scarce.

It was those parts of the relationship that I didn't want to admit to, but it became undeniably clear that Brian was just not that into me and certainly didn't love me.

I had been kidding myself, delaying my treatment in the hopes that this man would fall for me. The rose-tinted glasses were losing their effect; I knew I was walking forwards with my heart and not my head but foolishly continued to in the hope it wasn't true.

"Why do you let him treat you like that?" the girls

would say, exasperated. They felt he was not serious about me, but I was not ready to hear it. Instead, I would pull on the positives, like him getting me to help him add my feminine touches to his house. The two of us would go shopping for accents of colour or accessories to help transform his home to make it feel warm and less of a man cave.

But I knew it didn't outweigh things like the way I met his mum. Brian and I had been in the local hardware store again buying items for his house when we bumped into his mum there. It could not have been more awkward. It was like the cat had got Brian's tongue. I was stood waiting for him to make some kind of introduction, how embarrassing. His mother must have picked up on my discomfort and, in a bid to break the ice, made a beeline to introduce herself. It was far from an indication of Brian's commitment to me or us as a serious thing.

How could I not see it before? This was yet another sign that my friends were right about his lack of commitment. Feeling utterly disgraced, I told Brian to go on ahead with his mum while I lingered alone in the aisle by the plants, like an absolute no one.

A few days after the unwelcomed introduction, Brian's demeanour seemed to change. It was as though he had suddenly warmed to the possibility of an official relationship. He kept buzzing around me, excitedly commenting that now I had met his mother, he would have to ask her what she thought of me. What was the point of this, what was he trying to do here? Had he seriously had a change of heart or was he just playing with my emotions? His behaviour was very confusing to me –

he had blown cold and was now scolding hot. What had happened between then and now? Or what had been said between him and his mother? I wondered. It was quite a turnaround from the day at the store. I was trying so hard not to raise my hopes, I wanted to keep my feet on the ground, but hope kept rising inside me anyway.

It is so hard to dim down your reaction or response to someone when deep within yourself you are cheering and doing cartwheels. I wanted to be outwardly happy and excited, but I felt that I could not give the game away and show all my feelings.

I was so confused. Could this mean he did have feelings for me and wanted to get his mum's seal of approval? This was a 'situationship' that I could not read.

I did not press or enquire about the verdict from his mother. Instead, I tried to play it cool, though deep down inside, I was eager to know.

After he caught up with his mum, the verdict was in, and Brian was keen to share the news. The word was that I apparently had a good head on my shoulders and seemed nice.

All that fuss over a two-second review. I laughed to myself over how anxious I had been, but brief or not, it was positive, which was everything I could have hoped for. I thought back to my outfit choice that day and cringed. Had I known that we would see his mother, I would have chosen something a little more conservative than the playsuit and wedges I had on.

It struck me that after such a brief encounter, it would have been hard to arrive at the conclusion that I had a 'good head on my shoulders'; it seemed it was more likely

Brian's take, and his mum merely agreed. He then added that it would have been difficult for her not to like me in such a brief meeting.

Hearing this did not fill me with confidence. Instead, I began to wonder whether his mother could potentially be one of those mothers who see their sons as the ultimate prize and, therefore, are unable to see them as anything other than perfect.

*

Brian was due to travel for work. Travelling was part of his life, but when he was away, I missed him so much. Even though we spoke a few times a day, every day on video call, it did not change that for me. Nothing could match the connection of physically being with someone in person.

My doubts about Brian grew. I couldn't tell whether he was into me at all or simply filling his boots with sexual gratification. The more my friends picked apart the fragments of our not-quite-relationship status, the more I wanted to ignore it and remain in a daydream with only good outcomes.

The week he was away gave me more time to think about whether I wanted to go through with IVF. It felt like I was at a crossroads. I could have one or the other, but not both. I would have to decide soon.

It was a living torment. I was yearning to become a mother, have a family; if I was being honest with myself, I didn't want to throw that away because of a man. Yes, it was important to me to be a part of a family, to love and be loved, but at what cost? I had got so close to making a decision and now everything that I thought I knew or wanted was in question.

The curveball was that I loved this man, but if I could just unearth whether he loved me, it would change everything, because maybe I would choose him.

I could hear the voices of my friends play out in my head:

"Babes, you better mind because the way you two are sleeping together, any how you actually get pregnant and he doesn't want a child, it's going to be a madness."

"Have you even asked him if he wants children? You never know, he might want to support you through the IVF."

"Hun, you know what these musicians are like – he's probably got girls in every corner. He's a fuck boy."

"Cuz, I know a couple of guys who like you – why don't you just leave this sinking ship and see what's going on over there?"

The voices continued and got louder until I broke down in floods of tears. I shattered into a thousand pieces.

I wept face down on the floor and cried out to God:

"Heavenly father please help me, I don't know what to do. I love this man, but I'm also so scared. I don't know what to do. I'm not sure I can go through with the IVF anymore, but I still want a family; I am broken. I am barren! All I wanted was a baby; now he's come back into my life, and I've fallen for him. Please, if you could just fix my womb, I promise I will give the child back to you."

The day Brian was due back, we had planned that I would stay at his as normal for a few days. Now, standing at his door, I took a deep breath in and tried to gather myself. I had missed him so much and was excited to see him but didn't want to freak him out with the dramatics. As I knocked on his door, I had a sudden flutter of butterflies inside. It was unusual to feel nervous around him, but for the first time in forever, I acknowledged that this was the place I was at emotionally. I allowed myself to feel all the nervousness within me. My heart was quietly thumping faster in my chest. I took one last big breath.

Brian opened the door. I entered and he embraced me for what I wished could have been a lifetime as I sank into his arms. He kissed me, looked into my eyes and said, "I really missed you," and my heart skipped a beat.

This embrace felt different to all our other hugs; I felt like something was different about me too. Perhaps he had squeezed me too tight, because I realised my breasts felt so tender. *Great*, I thought, *my period is probably on its way*.

After catching up over our special brew, which consisted of a mix of loose tea leaves that he got from a Chinese herbalist shop, I excused myself to retire early and went upstairs. I was so drowsy I could barely stay awake.

The next morning, Brian was making breakfast of scrambled eggs and smoked salmon. I had not long come downstairs in my head-tie, his T-shirt and joggers.

"Oh gosh, can you please shut that fridge door, I just can't with the smell of that blue cheese," I said. We loved a good cheese board; I had tried to get Brian to understand the importance of having chutney to accompany it, which was taking a while for him to warm to. Though I really loved cheeses, I was not crazy for the blue kind like he was, I found the overpowering smell of them made me want to hurl.

As I sat down awaiting his carefully presented breakfast, he began to quiz me about how long we had been dating. His keen interest made me smile. It had only been three months, but as I sat there, I thought, *if every day feels like this when I am with you, I could honestly do forever*. And then, as though someone abruptly put a pin in my bubble, the doorbell went. It was his younger brother Alex.

Alex was quite a lively, loud character, quite a contrast to Brian, but it was cute to watch the love between the two brothers who were clearly also best friends. In and amongst their jesting, Brian walked across the room to where I sat and lovingly planted a kiss on my lips as though to reassure me.

It was normal for Alex to come over unannounced so I was already used to it, but I would have appreciated the slightest bit of warning so I could have abandoned the head-tie.

The three of us spoke about random things, just shooting the breeze, then Alex paused, glanced at me, and then the room, and asked what was different. He had noticed the changes I had made, the femininity that had been implanted by way of the splashes of colour in the chair cushions and tall plant that stood proudly holding position in the corner of the room. There was a further nod of the head from Alex and another glance to me, but I could not quite decipher if it was acknowledgement that he thought I'd be around for a while.

A few days later, Brian had to travel again. It had been two weeks since we'd seen each other as, unfortunately, once he came back, I started to feel rough and just chose to stay at home.

I was not someone who got sick often, but there were so many things that seemed to be off with me, I felt cause for concern so booked an appointment with the GP for the following week.

"Have you still not pooed yet?" Brian asked as he laughed.

It was the most annoying thing in the world; I felt so backed up. Had it not been for the other weird symptoms I was experiencing, I would have just gone and boiled some senna pods to help move things along. The most concerning thing for me was the tightness that I was feeling in my lower abdomen. It felt like my insides were being pulled and stretched; I was concerned that something was seriously wrong and that it was related to the multiple fibroids that I still had.

"I don't know why you didn't just get them to remove everything if they're still going to cause a problem; just ask for another surgery and get them to remove all of it," he said flippantly.

I did not appreciate Brian's input. He had no idea how hard I had found the recovery from the myomectomy, and though I had heard of a few people who had multiple surgeries because fibroids can grow back again, I could not think of anything worse than having to relive the trauma.

The day of my GP appointment could not have come sooner. After describing my varied symptoms, which also included vaginal dryness, I was given a urine collection pot.

As the doctor carried out the test of my urine in the same room with dipsticks, nothing could have prepared me for the news that was about to unfold.

"Everything seems to be normal, but you are pregnant."

"What!" I exclaimed in total shock. "I can't be, you must be mistaken, I can't have children – I have fertility issues – I need IVF to be able to..." I said, confused.

The doctor carried out the test again, and once more, just to be sure, but they all came back the same. I was pregnant.

I was in complete disbelief. Did I hear that right? How could this be happening? No, wait, how could this be happening! As the doctor came back over to where I was seated by her desk to fill out my notes, I had no choice but to acknowledge that this was really happening.

"Congratulations, this is fantastic news, especially as you had complications." The doctor beamed. She seemed happy for me, and I felt bad that I could not share her enthusiasm. Though I thanked her, my tone was low and expressionless. My head dropped with disappointment; I feared the timing of this was too soon for Brian.

At the same time, I could not deny that this was a miracle. It was a dream I never thought possible for me, at least not in this natural way. Even my gynaecologist had been convinced that I would remain childless. In what should have been a moment of unadulterated joy, I felt fear. I knew Brian would be livid. I just hoped that with time he would calm down and perhaps even warm to the idea.

I waited for two days after my appointment before meeting up with Brian. He picked me up in his car and we went to get a case for one of his instruments at a music shop, then continued on our way to get a bite to eat.

Both being a fan of Asian cuisine, we settled on an Asian restaurant. I signed into the restaurant's track and trace for us (a new system that was a consequence following the Covid-19 pandemic) as Brian hated the idea of being tracked. The waiter came and seated us at a table and, after a few minutes, he returned to take our order.

Brian was straight in there, wanting to know how my appointment had gone at the GP's.

I was not a good liar. I did not want him to probe me because I knew I would crack. This was hardly the place for such an intimate conversation. My hope was that we would speak once we got back to his house, but he was so insistent, and I was not managing to shrug off the conversation or redirect it to something else.

"Are you gonna tell me what they said?" he said, for the second time, slightly more irritated.

I felt like I was under a spotlight. I seemed to go still and mute. I had not had long to sit with the news myself; I had anticipated that he was not going to take it well, at least initially, I thought, but I wasn't ready to deal with a negative reaction.

My mouth went dry, and my heart was ten to the dozen. I was scared. No matter how the news was delivered, as soon as I said the words 'I am pregnant', our bubble would explode, and he would hit the roof.

As predicted, no sooner had those words left my mouth, there was an immediate shift in Brian's energy. For a moment he did not say anything, which for me was much worse than receiving his fury. I guess he needed to digest what I had just said. Then came the expected fury.

"How the fuck could this happen?" he said, seething but trying to lower his voice through gritted teeth in an attempt not to make a scene. I felt like responding with, 'how do you think?' but chose to refrain given how volatile the situation was. Stoking the fire with coal was not going to help.

The waiter had long come back with our dishes. In between side glances at me in annoyed disbelief, Brian continued to slurp away at his soup – he clearly had not lost his appetite. There were more moments of silence before he asked me if this was a prank. With every bit of seriousness, I told him that it was the absolute truth. The waiter returned to clear our plates, and I asked for the bill.

When the bill came, I felt compelled to ensure that my card was whipped out first – there was no way I was going to have him thinking I could not pay my way, especially not now. For the first time ever in any of our dining experiences, we went Dutch.

The drive home was painful. There was a huge wall of silence between us – neither of us uttered a single word all the way back to his house.

Once inside his house, he began darting up and down, furious and now able to fully express what had been pent up when we had been unable to speak freely. His rage came at me like bolts of lightning.

"How the fuck could this happen? I don't want to know about this – you have to get rid of it. The fact that we couldn't even communicate on the journey home is indicative of the fact that we might be okay in our bubble, but we're not equipped for this. We've only been dating for three months, if it was a year then fair enough, but you've not proved to me that you have my back or that you'll support me. We've not done enough of life together; we've not gone through any ups or downs to prove that we're strong enough to last. I don't want to have a kid with you. You just need to get rid of it. You can stay at mine when you get it done, but I'm telling you this is what needs to happen. I'm not going to have you come in here and put shame on me and my family; I'm not going to let you fuck up everything I've worked so hard for and all I'm trying to do," he raged.

There it was, I had just been puked up on violently by the guy I loved and who clearly did not reciprocate.

I sat there on the arm of the couch and took everything he had to say like a punching bag without saying a word. I was so full of anxiety that I could feel myself shaking, and I felt sick. As his words continued to spew out of his mouth, the reality of his reaction to the news woke me right out of the dream of us. Stupidly, I had thought that at some point, once he got out all his frustration, we would make up. But the more he ranted, the more I realised that was not going to happen. The penny dropped. Brian was dumping me off a cliff. We were over.

I should have known better than to decide to interject and defend myself, but it was too late. My defence was weak, and with me finally offering up information about wanting to try IVF, it only made me look like I had planned this whole thing.

He gave me this searing look as if to say I had set him up. The look was so cutting I could only acknowledge it from the corner of my eye. Had I been bold enough to look at him head on; his glare would have severed me into a thousand pieces.

I was devastated. But this feeling weighed more heavily because I also felt like a complete idiot. How could I have been so stupid at my big age to not face up to the signs that this guy was with me for a good time but not a long time? I had focused on the good elements within our relationship so much so that I deliberately chose to ignore the warning beacons.

Being such a hopeless romantic and dreamer are so typical of me – my friends often tease me for this, but they are equally protective because they know it often comes with heartbreak in the form of unrequited love.

I thought that by telling him that I wanted to see if I could go through with IVF, it would prove that my intentions had not been to trick him at all. I hoped he would see that I had wanted a donor so everything could be on my own terms, but instead, this had quite the opposite effect.

To Brian, it just provided him with proof of my intent to have a baby by any means available, including him. Now amid this emotional confusion, I too was doubting my intentions and was beginning to feel guilty.

I explained that I was not comfortable with the idea of a termination; I told him about my teenage pregnancy and decision to terminate and my subsequent vow to never go down that road again. I tried to help him understand my reasons for feeling this way. I confessed that I felt my fertility issues were punishment for what I had done. But it was all to no avail. He was not interested in hearing a bar of it and was certainly not sympathetic. As far as he was concerned, there was one solution to what he saw as a messy situation. A termination: simple and absolute.

In desperation, I tried another approach to appease him. "If you don't want this baby, you can just be the donor and I will never lumber you with the responsibility. You can just forget about us and get on with your life." I had not meant it to sound as cold and calculating as it may have come across, but in my mind, there was no way I could abort my baby. This little life inside me was a miracle, a literal one in a million. How could I be expected to tear away the life that I had prayed for?

I managed to talk him into letting me go home and having some time to think things through alone for twenty-four hours. I knew I did not need to think anything through – my mind was already made up – I was going to keep my baby. But for now, I needed to escape the intensity of the feeling of this pressure cooker situation.

Once I got home, I instinctively felt I needed to cuddle my stomach and talk to the life inside me. I felt the need to reassure my little one that whatever they may have heard, I loved them more than any words I could say and would do my best for them, for us. Even in such early stages of pregnancy, I was beginning to bond with my baby; I already wanted to shield them from the harshness of this world and the situation with Brian.

Being home was a relief; it enabled me to just breathe without feeling pressured into having a termination. My mind drifted back to my first pregnancy, how different that situation had been. I had been treated with love, supported by Matteo in my decision. Even though it was not what he wanted, and it hurt him deeply, he never actively villainised me or threw it back in my face. For the first time I realised that not every woman was as fortunate as I had been back then. I am sure at some moment in time we have all felt like our back was against the wall.

Despite this feeling, I understood that this was my body, and therefore the choices surrounding it were mine to make. What a mess of a situation, how on earth had things come to this, I tried to reason. Though this situation was far from ideal, I needed to refocus on some positive aspects in a bid to outweigh the negatives. I had a home; I had financial stability and a fighting chance to make a good life for me and my child. So, I tried to remind myself to keep on going the best way I knew how.

Brian had made it clear that he wanted to keep the pregnancy between us, so I honoured that. Twenty-four hours always sounds a lot longer than it can often feel in desperate situations; I knew it wouldn't be long before I would have to face Brian again. My mind raced.

I knew of girls who had dated their partners for a similar period as me, fallen pregnant, yet were warmly supported, so what was so wrong with me? Why wasn't I good enough to receive Brian's care and support? Did my history present me as damaged goods or low-hanging fruit? I couldn't tell. All the comments my friends had made, warning me about Brian, were ringing clear and true; perhaps he was just a 'fuck boy'.

The next evening, when the twenty-four hours were up, Brian called me. He wanted to know what I had decided and whether I was going to go ahead and book the clinic to have an abortion, but unfortunately for him, that was not going to be the case. Having had a bit of time to gather up some strength, I made it clear to him that I was keeping my baby.

To say he was not happy was an understatement, and In that very moment it felt as though my spirit was being crushed by the weight of his displeasure, which I could sense from his tone. Though I remained on the phone, a part of me was transported back in time to when I was a little girl, and my father would behave so cruelly. I knew back then only too well how quickly tempers escalated. Now, as a grown woman, any hint of a raised voice or threat would immediately send my stomach into a knot, and I would feel the back of my mouth become dry. The tiny hairs on my arms were standing on end anticipating danger. I froze, completely unable to react.

This reaction was not exclusive to a threat against me personally; it would still be as strong even if there was a verbal or physical threat to a perfect stranger. This type of confrontation even in fictional dramas was also triggering enough to have me in tears, unable to contain my emotions.

This scene that was being played out by Brian and I felt so intense I could almost feel as though a knife was being twisted in my heart. My heart that had once quickened its beats in the sheer longing for Brian was now on the floor; barely beating beneath his bloodied foot.

It has been said for as long as I can remember, that 'sticks and stones will break your bones but words will never harm you'. Whoever came up with that nonsense clearly had no comprehension of the effects of words negatively spoken and its impact.

This confrontation which is what this had most definitely become, had been slowing wearing me down, just as a piece of wood being filed over time by a rasp. I realised my body had become tense, so in a bid to quickly ease my discomfort I slammed the phone down. I didn't answer any more of his calls.

This was no longer just about me; I did not want to risk my baby picking up on my less than positive emotions. It was so important to me to do right by this precious and tiny human growing inside me as best as I could from here onwards.

I did not sleep a wink all night. I was shell-shocked. What I had considered home now seemed to lack warmth, and I felt alone and scared.

Checking my phone, I saw that I had a missed call from Paul and tried calling him back, but it went to voicemail. My phone started to ring – it was Brian. I answered, hoping he had dialled down the rage and was not going to call me out of my name.

I could not believe what I was hearing. After asking me not to speak to anyone about this, he was now informing me that he had spoken with his two brothers and told them everything. His older brother had, in turn, called my brother Paul and told him everything. I was stumped and felt betrayed.

How dare he do that and how dare his brother tell Paul. Clearly the missed call I had received from Paul was not of a social nature but instead to discuss my unexpected pregnancy. I hoped I was wrong, but I had a feeling which way that conversation was going to go.

Brian was a lot calmer, but I sensed he was choosing to take a different approach seeing as being forceful had not worked in his favour. He suggested we meet up and talk, but there was nothing to say that had not already been said, so I declined.

He then insisted on a video call. He did not want just a normal call because, in his words, he wanted to see me and look me in the eyes so, reluctantly, I agreed to speak in a few days. I knew this video call was going to be difficult; I needed time to gather whatever strength I had left to be able to cope.

The days that led up to the call had me in a frantic and anxious space. I had so many mixed feelings and emotions. I felt so guilty for wanting to keep my baby and for hurting Brian this way. But now it was clear he did not love me, in some small way it made it easier to focus on my decision and isolate my feelings for him somewhat. To love someone and know you were hurting them is excruciating, but so too was the realisation that he never loved me and wanted no parts of me and my unborn child.

When Paul finally called me back, he insisted that he wanted to hear my side of the story, but his leading questions, and the way he quizzed me, led me to believe differently. He stated that the game changers in this situation were that I had had an operation and had stopped eating meat and drinking alcohol to give myself a chance of having a baby through IVF, so it was obvious that my chances of fertility would have increased, and he proceeded to talk at me:

"To be honest, I appreciate your head is all over the place right now, and I am not surprised, because this situation is very awkward and uncomfortable. I know this is your situation, and I cannot tell you what to do with your life, but this problem has now landed on my lap. Brian's brother has been messaging me asking me if I have spoken to you; his mum is livid; and you are coming across like some crazy chick right now.

"Regardless if he never strapped up, you needed to take contraception too, because it's not like you didn't know you had this operation to give yourself a fighting chance of getting pregnant. You both should have strapped up to protect yourselves from STDs. Your little romance wasn't serious, and the way he is addressing you now, why would you want to bring a child into this world under those circumstances? I don't get it; do you not value yourself?

"The very fact they will have a grandchild, cousin, niece or nephew that is not going to be a part of their family. Imagine, if this situation goes ahead and Brian decides not to see his child. I will continue to see his brother and his family, and this topic will probably be brought up occasionally. This situation clearly bothers him and his family, and everyone is unhappy about it except for you. However, it's your life and you do what you got to do.

"It seems to me people are making decisions about the here and now and not thinking about the impact this has on the dynamic of our *family* but only what benefits themselves. This isn't how families behave, in my opinion. And you say that you want me to accept you as my sister. Karma is a bitch. You will end up on your own with your name as mud, with a baby. You need to ask yourself if this is what you want for your life. All you're doing is repeating generational curses.

"Even if what you have done is not calculated, you know your relationship was just a 'ting'. You need to focus on the positive side, which is that you got pregnant, and you need to have faith you can get pregnant again. You had an operation in March 2020; it's only been seven months, and I'm sure this will happen again.

"Look, this is stressing everyone out, so I can only imagine how you feel. But I'll be honest, you need to be prepared to be by yourself throughout everything, and remember… some random chick could have done this to me, and one day you may have a son or a daughter and God forbid this happens to them."

At the end of our call, I was floored. I could not believe that the sibling I had loved the most had turned his back on me for a friend.

I had become so invested in allowing myself to feel a part of Paul and his family, though in honesty, most of it was desperation on my part to just be loved and be a part of a unit. I thought we had built a bond and that he accepted me as his sister in the same way that I had automatically just embraced them all as family.

I feel silly to admit it, but I really felt proud to be his sister; it felt like a great badge of honour, but it now felt as if this badge was being ripped off in dishonour by him. I had never felt so distant from Paul.

In that moment, I felt so ashamed for having wanted to be a part of his family but even more foolish for thinking he could ever look past the fact that I was not biologically his sister, or family for that matter.

Over the years, because I wanted the happy ever after so much in a family setting, I had so easily allowed myself to believe that my brothers would be as accepting of me as I so quickly was of them. But with everything that Paul had just said, I could not help but wonder, had I been seen as *actual* family, he may have handled the situation differently.

I loved my brother Paul, but I knew that if he felt this way, then it was likely that the rest of our family would too and that there was a possibility that I would be cast aside as a huge disappointment.

It felt like I was in an impossible situation. If I aborted my baby I would forever live with the guilt and regret for doing something that would please Paul, Brian and his family, but not me. My name would still be mud, and I would still be hailed as the girl who tried to 'set him up'. So to that end, it felt as though my fate was already sealed.

I would also be breaking my promise to God, which meant so much to me to keep. I was far from perfect or holy, but this vow was important to me. And for what it was worth, I wanted to at least stay true to the parts that I could within my faith.

Being premenopausal meant my biological clock could stop at any second. I wished Paul would show more understanding of that and acknowledge there was no guarantee I would get another chance.

I honestly did not know if I would be able to carry a healthy baby to full term, and I suppose that was a real fear that pregnant women have in general, because you just never know. However, if God had enabled my womb to bring forth life, I did not want to disregard such a gift, irrespective of the circumstances surrounding it.

I told myself that Paul was only saying this out of anger or frustration over being placed in the middle of a mess he didn't make, one that could also negatively impact his business connections with Brian's family. Though I had empathy for him being put in a difficult position, it was gut-wrenching for me that he was throwing stones alongside Brian and his family. This was not about taking sides for me, but it seemed Paul had. And the side he had chosen was not mine.

*

I am in my living room propping up the cushions on the sofa. I add some additional ones in the spot where I will sit. In a bid not to have to get up again, apart from the predictable toilet runs, I have made myself a fresh cup of tea. My phone is on charge in preparation for my virtual counselling session that I have been looking forward to.

I have been so stressed by my continuous grapple with guilt. I am deeply anxious and recognise the signs that I could be falling into a depression. I can't let that happen – I owe you me at my best; I owe you the best of my love. I've learned that talking to someone can help to shift my perspective.

I need to make sense of the mess I have made by becoming pregnant. I need to make sense of why my whole life feels like a catalogue of self-made messes.

All I can think of is how unwelcomed my pregnancy is to everyone but me. I wanted you without question, so does that mean that I am guilty of setting Brian up? I know I never meant to bring you to life in this way, but nonetheless, I keep doubting how pure my intentions were.

You are a miracle I can barely believe is true

And I should be basking in this pregnancy, celebrating with baby showers and such. But instead, my mind has me paralysed on a series of events.

The last thing I remember reading from the consultant's report from Harley Street was that my ovaries were not reachable naturally. I held onto that so firmly that it was all I could see. Had I clung onto the wrong bit of information?

My session begins. I settle back into the sofa, readjusting the cushions behind my back. Day by day, you feel so much heavier in my womb that I wonder if I'm carrying the whole universe. Getting back up from this comfortable seat will not be an easy task.

"So why do you feel this is all your fault?" the counsellor asks.

"Everyone has pointed out how much I wanted a child – and I did!" I reply.

"Well, from what you have explained, he also knew you weren't on contraception. Doesn't it take two to make a baby?" the counsellor challenges.

"Yeah, but none of that matters. I told him I couldn't have children, and I didn't tell him I was planning to go forward for IVF. Now suddenly I'm pregnant, the optics are awful, even to me!" I explain.

I can't contain my emotions and I just burst into tears. I feel so lonely, but the heaviness inside my bones begins to lighten.

"I don't know if I can do this," I weep. "I don't even know if I deserve to be someone's mother. I'm on my own – should someone like me even be a mother?" I quiz.

"From all that you have told me, you have been through a very difficult past, but you have also done very well for yourself. You have been resilient, and you love your baby. Why shouldn't someone just like you be a mother?" reasons the counsellor.

Seven

Guilt

Here we are, you and me. You are busy fidgeting around inside me and I feel ready to burst. I have driven myself to the hospital for a last check-up before you and I finally meet in a few days. I waddle down the long 'green mile' corridor into the reception area and take a seat while I wait to see the midwife one last time.

The smell of cleaning products is overwhelming; it hits me in the eyes and makes my nasal hairs stand to attention. I close my eyes and drift away, imagining our first meeting. I wonder if we'll have an instant bond; I'm hoping you'll recognise my voice and my scent when I hold you.

My beautiful baby, you just won't stop fidgeting. I feel every move you make. We are way past the cute feeling of fluttering butterflies. I can feel how restricted the space is for both of us; I wince in discomfort as you push your foot right up against my abdominal wall like you're trying to break free. You are outgrowing your home at the speed of light; I am impatiently waiting to welcome you into this world.

"Oh, Maria, it's been such a pleasure being your midwife. I can't believe how quickly it's gone. I'll still see you for the home visits, but it will mostly be other midwives from the team," the midwife commented after being satisfied with all the checks.

"You've been so lovely. I've been lucky to have you as my midwife. Another pregnant friend of mine who lives in London hasn't been as fortunate to receive this level of care, so I'm grateful. Thank you for everything," I reply.

We leave the hospital. I take in this old world as I slowly walk back to the car. Our new chapter is on the horizon; it feels daunting, but I'm trying to be brave about the unknown one small step at a time.

I know I love you. This is the first time I have ever felt that I belong. This feels good.

*

Brian and I had our video call.

I had known that this conversation was going to be extremely difficult for me. My anxiety had risen through the roof in anticipation for this day once I had agreed to have this last call. As he joined the call and I heard his voice for the first time again in what seemed like an age, It struck me that I no longer knew this man. His manner was very forthright and stern. I felt my body begin to tense.

My heart quickened, and as fear began to bubble up inside me. I tried desperately to control my shallow breath, but I could still feel my heart pounding in my chest. I clenched my fist, desperate for something tangible to help me overcome this intense and impending feeling of doom, but my hands had become clammy to touch. Even my very palms were crying tears for me, and as if in agreeance my soul began to weep silently inside myself while the outer appearance of me tried to present calmness and control. The little parts of me as I once was with Brian began to ebb away.

It appeared that Brian had organised himself ahead of our video call, as he had presented a long list of questions to ask me. Awkwardness flushed over me, and I knew I was way out of my depths here. I could no longer hold my chain of thoughts together, and even if I had a valid point to raise in my defence, it felt like I was on the stand in a courtroom, and my cross examination was making me trip up on all of my words and stutter.

There were no civilities, he proceeded with his line of questioning.

When was my last period?

What were the dates of the previous months before that and what was their duration?

I had an app on my phone for many years which tracked my cycle; it had been a godsend because I was never good with recalling the dates of my irregular period. And given my issues with fibroids, it always helped to have that information to hand for any medical appointments.

He went on to say that he had carried out his own research that stated there are three strands of infertility; the first is your fallopian tubes being completely closed; the second that an injury or operation severed the chances to conceive; and the third, that it is difficult to conceive, therefore what may take some people two or three months, could in this instance take three or even five years of trying. He wanted absolute evidence to show that it was conclusive that I was infertile. He firmly let me know that he had reason to believe that this was not the case.

Why me, why did he even bother reconnecting with me if it was nothing more than fun? I lived two and a half hours away from London, so why didn't he just find a girl, any girl, within an easier distance to him? None of this was making any sense. I just could not get over the fact that in the cold light of day he saw me as nothing!

I felt so stupid to have even considered aborting my plans to have a child, in the hopes that we would live happily ever after. How foolish. I had put my hopes in a man over that of my dream to be a mother, yet here we were – nowhere – with my dream still in jeopardy.

With every word that Brian spoke, with every question and with every jab it felt like shots were being fired, and I could see with his next breath that he was already reloading.

I have met countless women who are single mothers. Their stories may not be identical to mine, but despite whatever personal heartache they carried, nothing was more important to them than loving their child. And that's exactly how I felt.

How could he assume to know what I was thinking or feeling? Of course, the circumstances surrounding my pregnancy bothered me.

Why was he negating his own responsibility in all this and the fact that I had told him I was not taking contraception? Surely, if I had really wanted to plan this whole thing, lying about contraception would have been the oldest trick in the book?

This onslaught was causing me internal pain, and that dreadful pain was far reaching. I was not just some girl he had liaised with on some drunken boys' night. It bothered me deeply that one day I would have to break my child's heart and tell them that their father did not want them. It bothered me that no matter how much I would douse my child in love and give them the best that I had, it could be cancelled out by the father-shaped hole in their life.

As much as I could not deny this situation was not ideal, the life growing inside me with not-yet-formed limbs, but with a steady heartbeat, was a blessing. And what I felt for them was already deeper than anything I had ever felt; it was beyond love and more far reaching than rejection. I needed to cling to the hope that all my love would be enough to cancel out the imperfections and keep us steady in the wind.

I told myself I had to get through this, but I was drained. Every second of the call felt like a minute; every minute felt like an unforgiving hour.

His comments stilled my breath. How could I take something that I did not know I had? The thing I was guilty of was losing hope, so much so that it didn't matter what details the doctors may or may not have said, all I could hear was infertility. And with each medical appointment, my despondence grew and grew into something immeasurable. Yes, I had hoped, begged and pleaded with

God to fix my womb. But I never knew my prayers had been answered until that fateful day in the GP's office.

The 'conversation' was sinking to lower and lower depths. In my opinion every child born into this world was innocent; and never could they be described as a bad omen. The utterance of those words left a bad taste in my mouth.

I had known Brian for twelve years, but I did not recognise the angry person glaring at me through the screen, spewing all these targeted words that burned through my flesh and broke my bones.

There was no let-up. I glanced at the timer that showed the duration of the call; what felt like hours and hours had in fact only been twenty minutes of question after question, statement after statement. I began to drift away, intermittently glancing off into the distance while he was mid-sentence. I wanted to be anywhere but there. I felt so detached from this version of us; I was on the outside looking in on someone who looked like me and someone who looked like him, trying to read the anguish written on their faces, concluding that whatever love story there once might have been had turned to ash and become this long goodbye.

I was beginning to accept defeat. I was not the victim in this situation; the combination of facts and vitriol that Brian had gathered up showed me as the perpetrator. I was not going to be heard. I was only going to be misunderstood. The trust between us had been severed.

That feeling of defeat was eerily familiar to one I once knew. It took me back to a darkness that engulfed my mood, my thoughts, my hopes and dreams and everything good I had ever known. That darkness had trapped me within its grasp summarily to a carnivorous plant. I was the insect who was cascading into the pitcher as the soil poured in like walls closing in, blocking out the light of hope.

Before the call, I had hoped that there might be a change of heart, that somehow there could still be a chance of a happily ever after for us. But above all, I hoped that this child could at least have two active parents.

All I knew now was that I would not lie to my child, but when the appropriate time came, I would do my best to handle sharing that information and holding space for their feelings with care.

Love was indeed a wicked game of loss. Though I was gaining my heart's desire of a child, I was losing the love I thought I had found. And now we were both lying in the separate beds we had made. I had brought this upon myself. The only way through this was to accept it as my just desserts.

Ever since the day I left my biological family home, Esther had never let me live it down. She had made it her business to tell me over and over that I had brought shame on the family. And furthermore, in her words, I was responsible for 'whatever it is that your father did or didn't do'. With every passing year that afforded me the chance to heal from that chapter of my life, I had also become convinced that I was to blame, that I was the cause of my father's behaviour towards me. The fault of my abuse lay with me. That was an unbearably painful weight to carry throughout my childhood, adolescence and beyond. In hindsight, I realise that not only in the case of Brian, but in other instances too, I had become quick to accept blame, whether that was something I made the other party aware of or not. But often, I would be the first to forgive, the first to apologise and the first to want to clear the air. I would come to the conclusion that in pretty much all cases, it was better to apologise, whether I was in the wrong or not.

I was sorry that this had happened and that he was hurt, but he wasn't the only one hurting. I too was in a lot of distress and had no one to alleviate it for me. I understood his anger towards me, but it gave him no right to treat me like I was something he'd stepped in.

"Why do you even want to be a mother when you don't have a family network to support you, do you just want someone to look after you when you're older? Are you doing this because you're lonely?" Brian questioned.

I was already drowning in fear and worry about what I was going to do – could I really do this motherhood thing alone? And now, to add to this tale of woe, I felt the betrayal of the two men I cared for most.

My family situation was not perfect, but show me a family that is. I had family outside of Paul, his brothers and our mum. Granted, I had not grown up with my biological family, so that meant that we had to work at developing our relationships.

The harsh reality of my fertility trouble was the worst way to realise the value of something you've got when it's gone. Once I was sure my fertility was gone, I needed to have a baby more than ever. I cannot adequately explain what it does to a person when you assume all your life that everything inside your body is in working order, only to be told that a part of your body has failed you. It changes how you feel about yourself. It makes you see the world differently. The frivolous things that you used to chase after quickly lose their value. It made me simplify my needs to love and family.

As happy as I was when people around me became pregnant, inwardly I would be distraught, torn apart by the thought that it was probably never going to happen for me. I needed my own bundle of joy, love and hope. I hated myself for having pangs of envy. I wanted to enthuse along with them, but each time I said the word 'congratulations', I could feel a lump of hopelessness rising in my throat, pushing down my tears.

Brian finally ended our call by informing me that he never wanted to see or hear from me ever again.

In the hours after the call, my nerves and emotions continued to scatter. I did not know what to do. I felt obliged to produce my medical records, yet I wrestled with the idea because I knew my records would not satisfy him. There was nothing a hundred per cent conclusive in the outline of my fertility. The conversations that I had had with the doctors were not *exactly* how the records read. And without that exacting specification that Brian demanded, he would still see me as a liar.

I was desperate for clarity of thought and emotions. I called Adrian. At first, I couldn't even get any words out. I just wept and wept and wept over the phone. Adrian consoled me. When I was done crying for a moment, I managed to give him an outline of the call with Brian. It didn't take long for Adrian to conclude and share how he felt I should proceed. It was agreed that the best thing to do was nothing at all. There was no point sending anything to Brian because if one thing was certain, he was not going to change his mind – he did not want to be a father to my child.

I never contacted Brian again. Neither would I ever on my own behalf. But should a day come when my child wants to know their father and make contact, I would never stand in the way. That would be their right and their choice; I would wholeheartedly support them no matter what.

My mind floated back to that dreaded evening I had told Brian of my pregnancy. I had expected anger, but there were a few of his words that had left their mark: "Don't even think you can ever come to my door and ask for anything," he said.

That alone had made me determined to ensure I provided for my child over and above anyone's expectation of a single parent. I did not want my child, who I had chosen, to ever feel as though they were disadvantaged. No matter what, I would work hard so we would never be without. I never wanted to find myself in a position where I had to crawl and beg Brian for help.

Another week rolled by. Paul was still giving me unsolicited updates on what Brian's family were saying. He let me know how poorly regarded I was by them. But he also had a specific message which he claimed came directly from Brian's older brother; he warned that I had better not try and take Brian's house, and I would not be getting any maintenance money.

I was beyond offended. No one had the right to assume I was after a payday. I may have been a lot of things, but a gold-digger was not one of them. All my life I had been self-sufficient and proud of that fact. I had got used to this weird paradox you find yourself in as an adult who was once a child of the state; when people knew of my background, I felt their expectations of me were markedly low or this exaggerated surprise at any achievement. Neither reaction was welcome by me, nonetheless, I was used to it. I was never interested in measuring myself against anyone else. In the most practical sense, I only ever wanted to afford food and shelter, to be okay and not be homeless or in debt. Of course, I had other hopes and dreams, but if I was able to provide for myself, that was a win.

It wasn't until my school friend Tameka made a passing comment years after we left school, 'you've done really well for yourself, better than me', that I took real stock of what I had achieved for the first time. Before that time, I had never had anyone acknowledge that I'd done well. I didn't realise until that moment just how much I appreciated being encouraged. I thanked my friend and held onto her words.

After all these years of depending on myself, that was not about to change now. I would not depend on anyone to help me support my child. Though I would be grateful for any emotional support, I knew it was going to be me, myself and I doing this motherhood thing.

In situations like this, it does not matter who you were seen to be before – I could have been Mother Teresa – no sooner had I made the decision to keep my baby, I was deemed a bad person. Someone who had deliberately sought out their victim and taken them down like a helpless lamb to the slaughter.

We're all human. And as humans we are prone to mess up multiple times. Although pure intentions can't always paper over the cracks our actions make, if they are taken into account, they can often absolve us from being deemed a bad person by ourselves or anyone else.

But beyond a mother's love for her child, that grace will not always be extended. Adulthood can be quite unforgiving of mistakes, leaving little room for you to remain a good person.

My mind was spinning with all the accusations and guilt. When Paul last spoke to me, he declared me a bad person. The thing that hurt the most with Paul is that he had given the impression that he was the only one in our family to have fully accepted me as a sibling, yet when push came to shove, he had dropped me like a hot potato. He had always spoken about family and its importance, yet here he was, publicly hanging me out to dry. But I guess his actions and words reflected the truth: he had never really seen me as family.

Paul's alliances were patently clear; my past instincts about his loyalties in regard to me versus his friends had come to fruition. Despite that instinct, I had let my defences down and leaned into trusting Paul. So, I felt even more stabbed in the heart when I found out he had been going around telling people I had set up his friend. He had also overstepped by way of telling our mum that I was pregnant before I had the opportunity to let her know. The dynamics of my relationship with Paul were forever changed for the worse. After all these years spent bonding, building a meaningful relationship as siblings, it had crumbled quicker than the time it took to build, and now we were headed towards being estranged.

But that's life. There was nothing left to do but accept the part I had played in everything. I accepted the way things looked from the outside looking in. If I didn't know my heart, know myself, I too would be looking at me sideways. It was a messy situation. Despite how emotionally beat up I was, I could not help but empathise with how Brian felt, because I genuinely cared for him. It was never my intention to hurt him, but I recognised that my choice was doing that.

Brian was right: I was guilty of wanting a child. I had prayed that my womb might be blessed and enabled once more to conceive. I was guilty of never believing I would get pregnant naturally. And I was guilty of withholding the fact that I was considering IVF and had adjusted my lifestyle after the myomectomy to improve my chances of success. Though I had not set out for Brian to be the father of my child, I had been recklessly carefree during our passionate moments so clearly open to the prospect by tempting fate a thousand times. I had failed him in lots of ways. Now I wished he would just put his arms around me and hold me close, but that wasn't going to happen, and so I accepted that this might actually be the last time I ever fell in love; I am far too unqualified for matters of the heart it seems.

I was guilty of trusting that Paul and Lisa would have my back despite having that deep-seated doubt so long ago.

It hurt in the worst way that the very people I had sought counsel from and confided in with the intimate intricacies of my fertility issues, plans and dilemma about disclosing all to Brian, were now nowhere to be seen. At least not on my side of the fence anyway. Paul had dismissed the part he played, thrown dirt on my name and still managed to keep his hands clean. And as Esther's words echoed around my head, 'people cannot be trusted', I needed to find a way to not let the anger eat away at my insides.

I was guilty for proceeding on the journey of motherhood despite the fact that it was clear Brian and his family did not approve.

There would be no escape from that guilt and shame; people would naturally enquire about my child's father time after time, forcing me to relive everything over and over again.

I knew I would be shouldering the burden of responsibility and the guilt of two people. I didn't know how my child would feel about me as their mother; would they lose respect for me, disown me or even hate me for bringing them into the world this way? I could only hope they would eventually apply discernment and mercy to two flawed humans; my decision to take parenting on alone and their father's decision to be absent.

Everyone seemed to assume that I was happy about the whole situation, perhaps secretly doing cartwheels because I was pregnant. As far as they were concerned, I had got what I came for. I had to accept that they would likely never understand the torment I felt. Though I already loved my child without question, so many people were displeased with my decision to keep my baby. That has been the dilemma since the moment I knew I was pregnant. The harsh reality of the situation dawning on me ensured I couldn't feel happy or joyous. Surges of guilt continued to disturb my peace and moments of gratitude for being able to defy the odds. How dare I feel grateful? I did not deserve to feel happiness when I had caused upset and distress to others.

Doing the right thing was like running a gauntlet, yet that was all I was trying to do. I was not prepared to kill something that was a part of me and a part of a guy that I felt stupid for loving.

I had fallen so hard for Brian and fallen so far from grace. I had become the girl who was wrong; I had become the girl who was despised. I had become the girl who had set him up.

Eight

The arrival

My beautiful baby was born in the month of May, a month that brings promise.

We had come out of a cold season in more ways than one, into the warmth of the sun and the beauty of blooming and flowers that push up through the grass.

The experience of becoming a mother when I thought I would never be one has been emotional beyond words. I could not be more grateful or honoured.

Your Uncle Adrian remained by my side, even at your birth, holding my hand tightly to remind me that I was not doing this alone. We both watched on eagerly as the doctor reached in and lifted you out through the small incision in my swollen abdomen.

Your bellowing cries bounced off the walls to signal your arrival. Here you were, demanding acknowledgement as the most important person in the room. And I could not have agreed more.

Though you had only been here for a few seconds

I already felt so proud of you; I tried to imagine how I would feel after a lifetime. Against the odds of my journey, you had arrived. You were perfect, my wildest dream come true. I just wanted to absorb the moment forever.

The nurse whisked you away to finish checking you: all ten fingers and ten toes, a strong heartbeat and the lungs of Luciano Pavarotti. It felt like time slowed down as I stretched my ears to hear every breath you took. I needed you back between my arms, getting acquainted with you on my chest. When the nurse brought you back to me a few seconds later, time settled into its usual rhythm. I marvelled at the splendour of your being and breathed in the hope of you as you took in your first suckles of milk.

*

Like the billions of humans who have gone through this rite of passage before me, you and I have become 'we'. For the first time in my life, I felt part of something much like a river becoming an ocean.

This is it: a new life completely dependent on me for survival – since conception – inside and now outside of my body. This is the scariest thing I've ever done, but I am ready to do everything possible and stare down anything impossible to meet your every need. These feelings bubbling around inside about this new reality already supersede how I ever imagined I'd be as a mother. In my youth, I had thought selfishly and superficially, that I would never breastfeed because I didn't want to end up with saggy breasts. Moreover, I was scared of losing the small breasts that I had. For years, I felt like less of a woman for having small boobs, which gave the appearance of a flat chest and meant that I could get away with not wearing a bra. You – my beautiful baby – have changed everything. You make me feel like more than a woman.

I know this is real, but it still feels so surreal. Though I have heard other parents describing a similar sentiment, nothing quite prepared me for this extreme love and protection I'm pouring over you. These past nine months, I have been riddled with guilt and despair. But your arrival – the arrival of true love – seems to have washed those awful feelings away. For now, at least.

I was so lost in you that I barely registered your Uncle Adrian cutting your cord, then congratulating me. "Well done," he whispered gently, "you did it." I had completed my mission impossible.

I carried you for nine months. Nine. Can you believe it? I struggled with severe girdle pain that left me doubting whether I would be able to safely and successfully continue the pregnancy at all. It felt like you were all in a rush to get out here into the world. Were you?

The fact that I had become pregnant with you so soon after having major surgery called into question whether my body had been given enough time to heal itself before carrying you.

I often found myself amid involuntary waves of panic that washed over me like hot flushes.

I was scared of losing you. You were already a massive part of me. And though you were not here yet, I could not imagine life without you.

You were a small little bump. A bump that, in certain outfits, was mistaken for me eating one too many cakes.

Admittedly, I felt smug about that. I was not one to frequent the gym, so the less weight I had to drop postpartum, the better.

My stress levels during the first trimester were sky high. I knew I was in need of extra support to bear the heavy weight of my situation, so I sought counselling to face off with my demons and exhale through the pain in lieu of your arrival.

The counselling sessions were virtual; we worked on coping strategies for present scenarios and potential future ones, like the reappearance of Brian, your father.

I have always been like a rabbit in the headlights when it comes to having difficult conversations or dealing with uncomfortable situations, so it was certainly best to prepare myself way in advance, one way or another.

I want you to know that I would never stand in his way or yours; if meeting each other is what you both desire, I would do my best to facilitate it. How could I deny either of you that connection and knowledge of self when I understand how important it is? I would only seek to confirm that it was a happy, healthy and safe relationship for you to have.

I continued to take stock of Brian's absence.

My close friends predicted that Brian would undoubtedly want to be a part of your life once you were out here in the world, but they had underestimated how strongly he felt and how committed he was to keeping his distance. My instincts told me that he would likely let the years fly past, so that he could bypass me and communicate with you directly once you had come of age. One can never predict how an older child or young adult may respond to meeting their absent parent. I fear that should Brian wait too long, he may not receive grace from you but instead be forced to accept resentment and unwillingness to form any type of relationship at all.

Despite the gift of holding you in my arms, I still have to pinch myself to believe that I am a mother. And despite the joy that motherhood brings, it is important to say that it has been far from easy. I still feel guilt creeping around under my skin, telling me that I am undeserving of this happiness.

You look more like your father than me, so when I see you, I see him. That is in no way a negative for me. But it does mean that, often, when I find myself stargazing inside your eyes, my mind will slip into wondering about what Brian might be thinking or feeling or even doing in that moment. Whether he is still as angry as the day he found out about you or whether he has mellowed. I wonder whether he would like to meet you but doesn't know how to take that first step towards you.

I know how much my decision hurt him, and that truly hurts me. What do you do when you find yourself at a crossroads, knowing that whatever you decide, someone you love will get hurt? I've been at that same crossroads before, only this time it was either Brian or me. The irony, of course, is that everybody gets hurt anyway. But the guilt, well, that's all mine.

I am the cause of Brian's pain, so when I look at you, I whisper prayers that he will forgive my choice, and me, and reach out so that you can know him for yourself. Given the opportunity, I think you will love him, just as I do.

*

After about four months, we began to settle into a kind of rhythm. Each morning I would say a prayer of thanks for my little miracle.

I did my best not to moan or complain about the lack of sleep or any discomfort I may have been feeling, because I had won the battle with Mother Nature.

The family, that Brian informed me I did not have, were around for support. As soon as we came home from the hospital, there were hands on deck. And though it was unconventional because neither of my parents were around to bask in those moments, the help was welcomed. I tried to push through the thoughts of what it would be like to share this with a mother. My mind drifted back to the day you were born – once I was back on the maternity ward, I called Esther. But instead of joy, she was vocal with her disappointment. She was disappointed that you were not her preferred gender. Even then, in my most shining moment, I was unable to please her. And it brought me back to being a little girl, being looked at disapprovingly and knowing, because Esther told me so, that I wasn't good enough because I was a shade darker than my father would have liked. I abruptly ended the call with Esther, unable to hold in my tears and the feeling of loneliness in my bones. I had to make a conscious effort to push down those emotions and focus my energy onto my baby. But my mind had other plans as it recalled Essie explaining to me, when I was a young girl, her reason for having me. She had been in 'The Mind House', which was supported accommodation, much like a hostel for those suffering with their mental health, long before I was born, and she figured if she had a baby, she could get out.

As a young child, it was devastating to hear that the reason for your existence was to be a tool used to escape an undesirable situation. That knowledge seeped into me and made me question my entire existence. I never want you to feel like a commodity.

Before you crowned me with the awe-encompassing title of your mama, I had always been a proactive woman – multitasking, goal setting and executing – and nothing has changed.

Five weeks after giving birth, we relocated. It is an understatement to say that was challenging. Throughout my pregnancy, Covid-19 was still rife, so it was pretty much you and me in a beautiful but isolated village. I was five months pregnant when we accepted an offer on our home – which happened quicker than I had anticipated – and I began packing our belongings into boxes in stages, room by room. We didn't have a new home to move to yet, but I had no idea what I would be like physically beyond that, so I dived in to make life easier further down the road.

A month later, I was filling up every Saturday with at least six property viewings for us to consider within the M25. That, too, was a massive undertaking, causing quite a logistical headache. We lived deep in the countryside in the east of England; my objective was to move closer to London for easier access for support from friends and family.

It took two and a half hours to arrive at my first viewing, at which point I had to beg the vendor to use the toilet before the viewing could even start. That desperation for the toilet became a pattern – of course it did, I was pregnant. Sometimes vendors obliged me and other times, to my horror, I was declined with a point-blank no. I mean, I was particular about sharing my bathroom space with anyone myself, so I completely understood people's apprehension about having a stranger use their toilet, but surely this didn't apply to a pregnant woman? But it did. There were times I'd have to find somewhere to squat – in built-up towns, in broad daylight – and it was less than dignified.

I soon cottoned on and purchased an essential travel accessory: a vintage potty. From that point on, to spare my blushes and avoid disaster, I went nowhere without it in the car.

If the first viewing was at 9am, it meant I would leave home at about 6am to arrive in time. Then, with a last viewing at 5pm, we wouldn't arrive back home until gone 7pm. It was exhausting, and I was getting tired of not finding exactly what I wanted for us or finding it and being turned down because I had a chain. Vendors were dragging their heels on decisions in the hope of creating a bidding war; I didn't have the patience or the time for any of it.

The weeks were closing in; I still hadn't found anything, and travelling across the country was taking its toll. I am the type of person who likes to be in control, but in this instance, I felt like I had none. Plus, our home was pretty much in boxes, so I couldn't do the usual things that an expectant mother would be doing: nesting and getting everything just right for your arrival. The seemingly endless stress of it was just too much. In the end, I resorted to viewing our home virtually and your Uncle Adrian made the viewing in person for us.

In my desperation to just get it done and ease my fear of becoming homeless, I put in an astronomical offer, which was of course accepted. Finally, I could breathe. At least now we had somewhere to go.

Over the next few weeks, our new home was alive with the chaos of builders, decorators and cleaners everywhere, making sure everything was as perfect as possible for you and me, and finally I was able to nest.

On moving-in day, my cousins drove up to collect us so I wouldn't have to drive. I spent the journey sitting beside you making sure you were okay, watching your chest rise and fall as you drifted in and out of sleep secured in your car seat.

Your Uncle Adrian met us at the other end. Having already picked up the keys, he unlocked the door of our new home and helped us settle in.

I'm not sure how settled one could be on an inflatable bed – that was my fate because none of our furniture could be delivered until a week later. So, night after night, for one week, I endured the misery of trying to sleep on this inflatable which would slowly deflate during the night and have me sleeping on the floor by morning. The risk of disturbing your sleep and hearing you cry your head off in annoyance at me pumping the air back in was not one I was prepared to take.

At four months old, you were dedicated. I had asked God for you and promised that if that miracle should happen, I would give you back to him. That was an emotional day for many reasons. I was full of joy at being gifted with you. But that joy was sitting on top of sadness; though extended family were there in force, I had no immediate representation by way of my father, my mother or siblings (my father had other children). My immediate family had become you.

From a weight of five pounds and some change, you kept on defying the parameters of centile lines set by man to predict your growth. I took that as an encouraging sign of things to come.

Just before you turned five months, I received the unexpected news that my father had passed away, which brought solidarity between myself and my half-siblings. Together we made decisions to organise his funeral; I mustered up the strength to prepare and deliver the eulogy.

Despite the painful history between my father and me, I did not hate him. I had long since received intensive therapy to eradicate the self-blame that I had carried for many years and had arrived at a place of understanding that that was who he was, and who he was had nothing to do with me.

For many years prior to that epiphany, it had taken for me to wind up in a bedridden state of clinical depression before I realised that I needed to confront those demons. I was grateful to receive professional help that enabled me to finally face them, make some sense of them and the darkness that had plagued me.

During the initial weeks of my depression, I honestly had no idea what it was. All I knew was how unhappy I was. All my life, I had fought to exist and fought to belong, but it all came to a head when I just didn't want to fight anymore. I felt so tired, so stuck and fed up of trying and trying and trying. My heart ached with pain and sorrow for a life I thought I would never have; a love I thought I would never know. I wasn't just alone without any immediate family; I was lonely. The world is a beautiful, miserable, enchanting and cold place. And I just didn't want to be here or anywhere. I didn't want to exist. Now, I think it's important to say that I never had suicidal thoughts, but I felt like I just wanted to be nothingness, as wild as that may sound.

My mother is a sick lady. I cannot blame her for anything, as much as I wanted to hold her, or someone, accountable for the things I had suffered in my early years. My father was just as sick, quite honestly. Now, I realise that when someone is so dependent on drugs to ignite their mood, they too are unwell. My younger brother and I had never really been afforded the opportunity to forge a real relationship under the watchful eye of Esther, so there was only ever just me.

My pastor would always say, "No man is an island," and he was right. I need somebody. You need somebody. We all need somebody. The story of my life meant that anyone in it was at some distance, physically or emotionally or both. Perhaps during my childhood, one night in my dreams, I built an invisible fence around me. And the moment I woke up, the memory of that just vanished, the way dreams often do. And perhaps I continued to grow into adulthood, longing for closeness but oblivious of that fence. Now, I felt that I had no immediate family to depend on.

Sometimes, people would show me glimpses of that

happy ever after, and I would cling to the idea of it, but it never came true. And each time, my heart would shatter.

How many times can your heart shatter before you lose the will to piece it back together, knowing it will be shattered again? I guess by design, it's infinite if you have breath in your body and the will to withstand the discouragement. But eventually, anybody's heart would beg them to give up, whisper to them to stop trying, until your mind and your body listen and stop functioning the way they always have. Instead, you stop caring. You fall down where you stand and just lay there like a lifeless body sprawled out in the middle of the road.

All these years, it hasn't felt like I have been strong at all. It's felt like I've been holding my breath and myself in and not allowing myself to feel anything as truly or deeply as I needed to. Every day became just another day to get through. I didn't recognise I was doing any of that at the time; it's only through the beneficial lens of hindsight that, suddenly, I see. Although there is a part of me that is ashamed that I gave up, I am grateful just to feel everything that has been shoved down.

During my episode of depression, I didn't want to be seen; I didn't want to see anybody, so much so that once I was home on long-term sickness from work, I would observe the neighbours' patterns to avoid them and their lines of questions about how I was and why I wasn't at work.

Everything that I had ever enjoyed before, I completely lost interest in. I used to be such a bookworm – I loved the smell of a book, the words and descriptiveness that unlocked your whole imagination, the sheer entertainment that its pages carried – but as the years have passed, I have lost the ability to pick up a book and read. And though I miss one of my favourite pastimes, I just can't seem to muster the zeal I once had.

Next, came the loss of appetite. Eating became such an effort – why on earth would I bother when I just didn't care? In a fleeting moment, it had crossed my mind as to why it didn't physically hurt – at that point I had not eaten for weeks on end – but I didn't care enough to dive into that thought. Eating became one less thing to be concerned about.

I did eventually book myself into rehab, which I oddly thought was cool because the likes of Amy Winehouse and Michael Jackson had apparently stayed at this facility.

I was also impressed that this rehab facility didn't smell like a ward or hospital, clinical and sterile, smothered in harsh chemicals that screamed bleach. Instead, this place had no distinctive smell and somehow felt like home.

The bedrooms were gorgeous, just like the ones you would expect to find in a four-star hotel. They were large double rooms, with a wardrobe, desk and an en-suite. There was a fully kitted-out gym on site, which even seemed to appeal to me.

The restaurant was a bit canteen-ish, but the food was far from a school dinner. The chef must have been worth every penny they were paid because the sweet smell of herbs and seasonings they had wafting from the kitchen on a daily basis beckoned to my senses and slowly encouraged me to start eating again.

Every day was scheduled like a school day; you had classes and therapy sessions to attend throughout. The first day I attended a session, I felt daunted by the prospect of having to share a space and my private thoughts with an audience of strangers who had also given up and found themselves there.

Soon enough, I felt relatively comfortable there because everyone was as vulnerable as me, so it felt normal. But you could feel the extreme sadness and the weight of their souls as soon as you entered a session. The air was thick with worry and despair and hopelessness. Within these sessions, we were immersed in a lot of CBT; it was like getting a factory reset for our minds, switching them from one way of thinking to another. And then, as we developed over time, we were able to question ourselves as to why we thought so negatively about whatever it was and to replace that with something positive.

Honestly, I really struggled with the group sessions because, I had always been such a private person. With hindsight, I can see that sharing and listening to others was the type of healing I could not have experienced in one-to-one sessions. After such long days of various group sessions, the crescendo for me was the mindfulness classes which always seemed fitting and relaxing at the end of a full day. I had been a little weary of participating because of my Christian background; the fact that its practices were taken from a different faith made me feel conflicted, but it helped me feel at ease. I could feel all my cares just floating away; it was the first time that I had felt a real sense of being able to let go. It was a breakthrough because I was finally able to separate myself from my worries and strife. We were no longer one – I was me, and my cares were totally separate from me.

Each beat of the brass bong in a mindfulness session enabled me to drift into a cloud of peace. A cloud where there were no cares, worries or concerns but simply balance and pure peace.

Bong! The sound of that beat of the brass carried me further away, away somewhere safe that I wish I had found in my own life. And as my breathing steadied, my eyelids would close as I drifted into sleep.

During my time in rehab, I met some lovely people. They were people who had, in one way or another, been slapped in the face by life, and the effects had shown themselves through eating disorders, depression and suicide attempts.

Within my large group of depressed individuals were people who held a variety of roles across various fields; there were managing directors and people from banking and marketing. No matter our backgrounds, we committed to attending our sessions, divulging deep feelings that perhaps we had not even realised we had before that point. We bonded; we determined to support each other as much as we would support ourselves. The level of commitment to each other was huge, considering we had little strength to prop our own selves up.

One evening, I had been preparing for bed, pottering about in my room in nothing more than my smalls and a bra, when my bedroom door flew open. I was horrified and felt violated.

I screamed at the male nurse, spitting a surge of anger at them for daring to open a closed door without knocking. Their response was unmoved, which further angered me. They didn't see what all the fuss was about as they were just doing their round of checks for the evening.

For the first time I realised that I was angry, not only that, but angry at men who I felt overstepped their position and put me in a compromised and vulnerable position. That was also the first time that I had ever been able to use my voice. I made my voice audible enough to be heard in the face of what I saw as a threat. All other times I had felt paralysed, frozen and unable to move or make a sound, as though my limbs had stopped working and my voice box had been torn from my throat. In the throes of a threat, it was like I had left my body and my soul was hovering over me, watching but unable to do anything to help.

That night I complained to the night staff. I was never the type of person to complain, I was used to bearing a lot, but something inside me was beginning to change. I was becoming less agreeable to B.S. and that was a good thing.

That evening I found it very difficult to settle. I stirred, unable to find comfort in the sheets I had pulled right up to my neck for comfort. My door was locked from the inside, but the effects of being walked in on had me pushing the desk chair up against the door. That way, even if I fell asleep, nobody could enter without inadvertently alerting me to their presence.

That night was long; it left my mind trailing back to my parents. Deep down inside of me, I always felt like I hadn't quite been enough, that I'd somehow missed the mark. It was confusing how Esther could on the one hand consider me a good child, yet on the other, blame me for my father's indiscretions. As for my father, I didn't know what his opinions were of me aside from being disgusted that I would dare to accuse him of something as hideous as abuse.

I couldn't sleep; my mind just refused to rest, turning and re-turning, piecing memories together, then breaking them apart before piecing them back together over and over again.

Ours was a family always on the edge. When my parents would fall out, quarrelling and fighting with their words, it quickly became white noise. But every now and then, they would launch a set of words that broke through the monotony like weapons of mass destruction: "She's not mine!" said my father, referring to me. I wonder if he ever considered the impact of his words or his actions on me. But as I lay sleepless in my bed, staring up at the ceiling, I just felt sorry for him. I was sorry for the man that was my father, sorry that he could choose such low blows and aim them at my mother and at me, his child, just so he could win the round in those wars of words.

How sad it was that between them they had created such a toxic environment. I couldn't help but pity them both. In many ways, they were no different from any other parent, ill-equipped right from the start. I know now that neither of them were capable of acknowledging their faults, let alone apologising for them. They were both wrong and strong. And no child would have been permitted to tell them any different.

For me, it felt like an easier task to forgive my father rather than Esther. The difference was that Esther had blamed me and not protected me as I felt she should have. She had chosen to sweep things under the rug as though it was okay, but on her own terms, she would bring up these painful things from the past whenever she saw me and throw salt in my wounds.

Esther has not forgiven me for running away from home, never returning and, in her words, bringing shame on the family. And I know she never will.

I always imagined that in years to come I would willingly help my father should he need help in his old age. Now, organising his funeral and preparing his eulogy was the only help I could offer him.

After my father's send-off, the emotions of everything hit me. Waves of grief engulfed me as I tried to make sense of it all.

I was incredibly sad at the way he had passed, more so at the way things had been, things that could never be changed.

I was grieving the death of this part of me; despite it all, he was still my flesh and blood. I was grieving the father that could have been but was not. And I was grieving the fact that he did not have the pleasure of meeting his grandchild before leaving this earth.

Now you were here, I determined to put my best foot forward and start as I meant to go on. We began attending weekly mum and baby workouts, baby groups and lunches.

It was at these lunches and other activities that I noticed my forehead and chest would break out in beads of sweat. Those beads would soak through my clothes. Even with the reoccurrence of this, it was not until someone jokingly commented that surely I could not be going through 'the change', that I considered it for a second.

But that theory would quickly be swept away by someone else mentioning the fact that I had just had a baby. Of course, I would conclude that it was completely normal for my hormones to be all over the place.

But the thought wouldn't quite rest. Some time after, I started to consider the prognosis that had been given to me at Harley Street, specifically outlining that I was premenopausal.

As you do, I turned to Google. I searched for a rational explanation to put my thought to bed, but of course, it threw up more questions. According to everything I read, my hormones should have balanced out within weeks, not months, of giving birth.

So, I decided to err on the side of caution and book an appointment with the GP. Once I explained my concern, the doctor decided that the best course of action was to do some blood tests to make sure there was nothing untoward happening.

By the following week, my results came back, and the doctor was surprised at the findings. My blood work had confirmed that I was not premenopausal but that my menopause had commenced. This was rare for someone so soon after childbirth and of my age – I was forty. So, just to be sure, the blood tests were run again. For the second time, the results showed, without a shadow of a doubt, that I had reached menopause.

Just six months after having my baby, the warning bells telling me to follow my gut instincts had come to fruition.

That slight gape of the door that Mother Nature had shown me was my last chance to bear a child. I took that chance; my prayer was granted; then the door was firmly closed.

All these months of persecution and finger-pointing, self-doubt and self-blame, chastising myself for wronging Brian. Dealing with the betrayal of Paul and being outcast.

The hell I was going through and the will I had to muster to keep going through it, has led me here. Paul and others had been so hung up on my fibroids and the operation I had to remove them that no thought had been given to the other issue surrounding my infertility.

Fibroids was something that people had heard of, so they felt comfortable in offering up opinions about it and fertility in general.

Being premenopausal seemed too far-fetched for someone who was not even in their fifties. I recall telling Brian when he had asked about the details of my infertility, and he had just shrugged it off as though I was being preposterous.

Here we are, I am a new mother with a beautiful baby. Everything that I went through was unwelcome but worth it. I could never take back even a single second of any of it and risk a different outcome, never in a billion years. It was my choice to have my baby, the consequences were not.

It's kind of fun to think about how twenty-something me would react to this version of myself. Back then, I had no room for children. I was footloose and fancy-free. The only thing I was interested in was getting myself on the property ladder, maintaining a good job and looking flawless.

Life will always find a way of making things fall apart before reimagining them and piecing them back together. My child will soon be three years old. I have had no contact or enquiries from Brian. I can only assume that he has been made aware that I had the baby, but he is unaware of everything in between and missing out on this new life with you in the world.

I have no idea whether that will always remain, whether Brian is content in waiting to see if our child is interested in meeting the other person whose DNA they carry. But irrespective of that, my love for Brian will always remain because he imparted a priceless gift. A gift that I will always be thankful for.

*

Happy birthday to you, my darling 'Peanut'.

It's a beautiful day in May; sunbeams flood our home with warm light. The living room is packed full of family members here to celebrate you. Throughout your first year of life, you and I have faced so many highs and lows together – first steps, sleepless nights, grief – our bond is unbreakable. I have learned many things from motherhood about love and family and gained a new understanding about what it means to be alone. Yes, I am raising you alone, but I do have people – family – who have and will show up and show out for me, for us.

The love around us and between us is tangible. You are being carried from hand to hand, in the arms of aunties, uncles, cousins – you are cherished and praised. We are in our element as reggae music plays amid clinking glasses and laughter. It's one of those days when your cup is so full that you wonder if it is possible for life to get any better than this.

There have been excruciating times when I felt like I was walking through valleys with bare feet on broken glass, full of uncertainty and self-loathing. But somehow, despite it all, I stood in my convictions and kept going.

Here we are, you and me and our family. I have given myself permission to be happy and enjoy you; it takes the sting out of the pain when my mind hovers on those not present: my mother, my father and Brian. Now, I am too grateful for life to allow their absence to steal my joy.

The dust may still be settling over the circumstances of my unexpected pregnancy, but you, my precious child, are the single most important achievement of my life. This is where you begin. You were always destined to be here – God has so many things to show you.

This book is printed on paper from sustainable sources managed under the Forest Stewardship Council (FSC) scheme.

It has been printed in the UK to reduce transportation miles and their impact upon the environment.

For every new title that Troubador publishes, we plant a tree to offset CO_2, partnering with the More Trees scheme.

MORE TREES
LET'S PLANT A BILLION TREES

For more about how Troubador offsets its environmental impact, see www.troubador.co.uk/sustainability-and-community

Taste

THE ITALIAN LIST

Giorgio Agamben

Taste

TRANSLATED BY COOPER FRANCIS

LONDON NEW YORK CALCUTTA

The translation of this work has been funded by SEPS
SEGRETARIATO EUROPEO PER LE PUBBLICAZIONI SCIENTIFICHE

S·E·P·S
SEGRETARIATO EUROPEO PER LE PUBBLICAZIONI SCIENTIFICHE

Via Val d'Aposa 7, 40123 Bologna, Italy
www.seps.it

The Italian List
SERIES EDITOR: ALBERTO TOSCANO

Seagull Books, 2017

Giorgio Agamben, *Gusto* © Quodlibet, 2015

English Translation © Cooper Francis, 2017
First published in English by Seagull Books, 2017

ISBN 978 0 8574 2 436 5

British Library Cataloguing-in-Publication Data
A catalogue record for this book is available from the British Library

Typeset by Seagull Books, Calcutta, India
Printed and bound by Maple Press, York, Pennsylvania, USA

CONTENTS

1
Taste

79
Notes

TASTE

1. *Science and Pleasure*

Contrary to the privileged stature that has been granted to sight and hearing, the Western cultural tradition classifies taste as the lowest of the senses, whose pleasures unite man with other animals and in whose impressions one will not find 'anything moral'.[1] Even in Hegel's *Aesthetics* (1817–29), taste is opposed to the two 'theoretical' senses, sight and hearing, since 'a work of art cannot be tasted as such, because taste does not leave its object free and independent, but deals with it in a really practical way, dissolving and consuming it'.[2] On the other hand, in Greek, Latin and other modern languages derived from them, there is also a vocabulary that is etymologically and semantically connected with the sphere of taste which designates the act of knowledge: 'The word "sapiens" [wise man] is derived from "sapor" [taste] (*Sapiens dictus a sapore*) for just as the sense of taste is able to discern the flavours [*sapore*] of different foods, so too is the wise man able to discern objects and their causes since he recognizes each one as distinct and is able to judge them with an instinct for truth,' we hear in a twelfth-century etymology by Isidoro de Sevilla.[3] Similarly, in his lesson of 1872 on the pre-Platonic philosophers, the young philologist Nietzsche noted the following with respect to the Greek word *sophos*, 'sage': 'Etymologically it relates to the family of *sapio*, taste; *sapiens*, the taster; *saphes*, perceptible to taste. We speak of taste in art: for the Greeks, the image of taste is considerably expanded. A form redoubled as in *Sisyphos*, of strong taste (active); even *sucus* pertains to this family.'[4]

In the course of the seventeenth and eighteenth centuries, authors began to distinguish a faculty that proclaimed the judgement on and enjoyment of the beautiful as its specific concern. It is in fact the term 'taste' that, in the majority of European languages, takes on a metaphorically opposite and additional sense so as to indicate this special form of knowledge that enjoys the beautiful object and the special form of pleasure that judges beauty. On the first page of the *Critique of the*

GIORGIO AGAMBEN

Power of Judgement (1790), Kant describes with his usual lucidity the 'enigma' of taste as an intertwining of knowledge and pleasure. In a discussion on the judgement of taste he writes:

> For although [these judgements] contribute nothing at all to the knowledge of things, still they belong to the faculty of knowledge alone, and prove an immediate relation of this faculty to the feeling of pleasure . . . [this relation] is precisely what is enigmatic in the principle of the power of judgement.[5]

From beginning to end, the problem of taste thus presents itself as that of 'another knowledge' (a knowledge that cannot account for its judgements but, rather, enjoys them; or, in the words of Montesquieu, 'the quick and exquisite application of rules that we do not even know'[6]) and of 'another pleasure' (a pleasure that knows and judges, as is implicit in Montesquieu's definition '*mesure du plaisir*'): the knowledge of pleasure, indeed, or the pleasure of knowledge, if in the two expressions one gives the genitive a subjective and not only objective value.

Beginning with Alexander Gottlieb Baumgarten, modern aesthetics has developed as an attempt to investigate the particularity of this 'other knowledge' and to establish its autonomy alongside intellectual cognition (*cognitio sensitiva* alongside *logica*, 'intuition' alongside 'concept'). In this manner, setting out the relation as one between two autonomous forms within the same gnoseological process, aesthetics left untouched the fundamental problem that, as such, ought to have been

GIORGIO AGAMBEN

investigated: Why is knowledge originally divided and why does it maintain, likewise originally, a relation with the doctrine of pleasure, that is, with ethics? Is it possible to reconcile this fracture—that science knows the truth but cannot enjoy it, and that taste enjoys beauty, without being able to explain it? Is it possible that science could be the 'pleasure of knowledge'? How can knowledge enjoy (taste)? Considering aesthetics in its traditional sense to be a historically closed field, we instead propose in the present study to position taste as the privileged site to illuminate these fractures that essentially characterize Western metaphysics—both the division of the epistemic object into truth and beauty, and the division of human ethical *telos* (which in the Aristotelian ethics still appears undivided in the notion of a *theoria* that is also *teleia eudaimonia*, 'perfect happiness') into knowledge and pleasure. In the

TASTE

Platonic formulation, these fractures are so originary one could say that they constitute Western thought not as *sophia* [wisdom] but as *philo-sophia* [love of wisdom]. Only because truth and beauty are originally split, only because thought cannot integrally possess its proper object, can it become the love of wisdom—that is, philosophy.

2. Truth and Beauty

In the *Phaedrus*, Plato establishes the differential status of beauty with the assertion that, while wisdom has no perceptible image, beauty has the privilege of being the most visible:

> Beauty, as I said before, shone in brilliance among those visions; and since we came to earth

we have found it shining most clearly through the clearest of our senses; for sight is the sharpest of the physical senses, though wisdom is not seen by it (*phronesis ouch horatai*). For wisdom would arouse terrible love, if such a clear image (*eidolon*) of it were granted as would come through sight, and the same is true of the other lovely realities; but beauty alone has this privilege, and therefore it is most clearly seen (*ekphanestaton*) and the loveliest (*erasmiotaton*).[7]

In the lack of an *eidolon* for wisdom and in the particular visibility of beauty, what is at play is thus the original metaphysical problem of the fracture between the visible and the invisible, or appearance and being. The paradox of the Platonic definition of the beautiful is the visibility of the invisible or the sensible appearance

TASTE

of the Idea. Yet, it is this very paradox that offers both the foundation and motivation for the Platonic theory of love—and in this precise context, the problem of the beautiful is developed in the *Phaedrus*.

The visibility of the Idea in beauty is, in fact, the origin of the amorous mania that the *Phaedrus* always describes in terms of the gaze and the epistemic process that it brings into being, whose itinerary Plato establishes in the *Symposium*. There, he characterizes Eros' stature in the epistemic realm as a medium between wisdom and ignorance and, in this way, compares it to true opinion, knowledge that judges correctly and grasps the truth without, however, being able to justify itself. Indeed, this medial character of Eros is the basis of its identification with philosophy:

GIORGIO AGAMBEN

Have you not observed that there is something halfway between wisdom and ignorance?' 'What is that?' 'Right opinion (*orthe doxa*) which, as you know, being incapable of giving a reason (*logon dounai*), is not knowledge—for how can knowledge be devoid of reason?—nor again, ignorance—for neither can ignorance attain the truth—, but is clearly something which is a medium between ignorance and wisdom (*metaxy phroneseos kai amathias*).[8]

[. . .]

[Love] is a medium between ignorance and knowledge. The truth of the matter is this: no god is a philosopher or seeker after wisdom, for he is wise already; nor does any man who is wise seek after wisdom. For herein is the evil of ignorance, that he who is neither good nor wise is nevertheless satisfied with himself: he has no desire for that of which he feels no want.' 'But who then, Diotima, are the lovers of wisdom, if they are neither the wise nor the foolish?' 'A child may answer that question,' she replied, 'they are those who are in a mean between the two; Love is one of them. For wisdom is a most beautiful thing and Love is of the beautiful; and, therefore, Love is also a philosopher or lover of wisdom, and being a lover of wisdom is in a mean between the wise and the ignorant.[9]

Each time it appears in the *Symposium*, the amorous trajectory is described as a process that goes from the vision of a beautiful body to the science of beauty (*tou kalou mathema*) and, finally, to the beautiful as such, which is now neither body nor science:

> Nor again will our initiate find the beautiful presented to him in the guise of a face or of hands or any other portion of the body, nor as a particular description or piece of knowledge, nor as existing somewhere in another substance, such as an animal or the earth or sky or any other thing; but existing ever in singularity of form independent by itself.[10]

The paradoxical task that Plato assigns to the theory of love is, therefore, that of guaranteeing the relation (the unity as well as the difference) between beauty and truth, or between that which is most visible and the invisible evidence of the Idea. In fact, the principle

TASTE

according to which the visible (and therefore the beautiful as 'that which is most apparent') is excluded from the domain of science is among the most profound intentions of Platonic thought. In Book 7 of the *Republic*, Plato explicitly affirms that it is impossible to grasp the truth of astronomy from the standpoint of appearance and visible beauty. The beautiful varieties of the celestial constellations cannot be, *as such*, the object of science:

> These sparks that paint the sky, since they are decorations on a visible surface, we must regard, to be sure, as the fairest and most exact of material things but we must recognize that they fall far short of the truth, the movements, namely, of real speed and real slowness in true number and in all true figures both in relation to one another . . . Then, I continued, we must

use the blazonry of the heavens as patterns to aid in the study of those realities, just as one would do who chanced upon diagrams drawn with special care and elaboration by Daedalus or some other craftsman or painter. For anyone acquainted with geometry who saw such designs would admit the beauty of the workmanship, but would think it absurd to examine them seriously in the expectation of finding in them the absolute truth with regard to equals or doubles or any other ratio.[11]

Formulating in a certain manner the programme of the exact sciences, Simplicio is right to claim in his commentary on Aristotle's *On the Heavens* that the foremost intent of the Platonic *episteme* is a *ta phainomena sozein*, a 'salvation of appearances': 'here is the problem that Plato offered to researchers in this field (astronomy): to find those circular and perfectly regular movements, there is a need for conjecture in order to save the presented appearance of errant stars.'[12] Yet only if one could found a knowledge of appearances as such (that is, a science of visible beauty), would it be possible to truly 'save the phenomena'. The *episteme*, by itself, cannot 'save appearances' in mathematical relationships without presuming to have exhausted the visible phenomena in its beauty.

It is for this reason that the relationship between truth and beauty is the centre of the Platonic theory of Ideas. Beauty cannot be known and truth cannot be seen—yet it is this very intertwining of a double impossibility that defines the Idea and the authentic salvation of appearances in Eros' 'other knowledge'. In fact, the

GIORGIO AGAMBEN

significance of the term 'Idea' (with its implicit etymological reference to an e-vidence, to an *idein*) is entirely contained in the play (in the unity–difference) between truth and beauty. Thus it is that, in the dialogues on love, every time one appears to be able to grasp beauty, there is a return to the invisible; every time that one appears to be able to close in on the consistency of the truth through *episteme*, there is a return to the vocabulary of vision, seeing and appearing. Only because the supreme act of knowledge is split in this manner into truth and beauty ('wisdom is knowledge of the most beautiful' and the beautiful is 'that which is most apparent', but science is 'science of the invisible'), wisdom must be constituted as 'love of knowledge' or the 'knowledge of love' and, beyond any sensible knowledge as much as *episteme*, must present itself as philosophy. That is, as a medium between science and ignorance—between a having and a not-having.

From this perspective, it is significant that the *Symposium* attributes the sphere of divination to Eros. This is because divination is precisely a form of 'mania': knowledge that cannot, as with *episteme*, explain itself or phenomena but, rather, concerns that which in them is simply sign and appearance. The contraposition between the *orthe mania* of love's knowledge and *episteme* leads once more to the Platonic attempt to institute 'another knowledge' and to save the phenomena between the invisibility of the evidence (truth) and the evidence of the invisible (beauty).

Yet, the Platonic theory of love is not just a theory of another knowledge but also the theory of 'another pleasure'. If love is in fact the desire to possess the beautiful,[13] if to possess the beautiful is to be happy (*eudaimon estai*), and if love is, as we have seen, love of knowledge, then the problem of pleasure and that of knowledge are strictly connected. For this reason, it is certainly not an accident that, in the *Philebus*, pleasure is analysed from the perspective of science, and that the supreme good is identified as a mixture (*synkrasis*) of science and pleasure, truth and beauty. Plato distinguishes, here, the pure pleasures (*hedonai katharai*)—those of beautiful colours, of figure, of certain odours and sounds—that can be intertwined with science, from the impure pleasures which do not tolerate any relation with knowledge. The mixture of the pure pleasures and pure science is, however, explicitly characterized as the work of beauty, such that the supreme object of pleasure as of science takes refuge once again in the beautiful ('thus the power of the good . . . it takes refuge in the nature of the good'[14]). The fracture of knowledge that Plato leaves as an inheritance to Western culture is, therefore, also a fracture in pleasure. Yet, both of these fractures that originarily characterize Western metaphysics signal towards an intermediate dimension in which one finds the demonic figure of Eros, who appears to be the only one capable of effecting conciliation without thereby abolishing difference.

Only by placing oneself upon such a foundation —that is, only if one can account for this complex metaphysical inheritance, pregnant with the science that, since the end of the eighteenth century, ingeniously presents itself both as 'science of the beautiful' and 'doctrine of taste'—will it be possible to formulate in adequate terms the aesthetic problem of taste. That is, only on such ground can one grasp that taste is at the same time a problem of knowledge and pleasure or, rather, in the words of Kant, the problem of the 'enigmatic' relation between knowledge and pleasure.

3. *Knowledge that Enjoys and Pleasure that Knows*

The formation of the concept of taste, from the beginning of the sixteenth century until its final enunciation in the many eighteenth-century treatises on taste and the beautiful, betrays its metaphysical origin through the secret solidarity it presupposes between science and pleasure. Taste appears from the beginning as a 'knowledge that does not know, but enjoys' and as a 'pleasure that knows'. It is thus not a coincidence if, as Robert Klein demonstrated, the first appearances of this

TASTE

concept are more often to be found in treatises on love and in magico-hermeneutic literature than in artistic literature, strictly speaking.[15] It is in a passage from Book 16 of Campanella's *Theologia* (1613–24) where, in a discussion on the influence of angels and demons on man, we find one of the most untimely appearances of the gustatory metaphor used to signify a particular form of immediate cognition:

> *Non enim discurrendo cognoscit vir spiritualis utrum daemon an angelus . . . sibi suadet . . . aliquid; sed quodam quasi tactu et gustu et intuitiva notitia . . . quemadmodum lingua statim discernimus saporem vini et panis.*

> It is not by deliberation that man judges whether a spirit is a devil or an angel . . . It is rather by sensitivity and an intuitive understanding

that he is persuaded . . . just as we immediately recognize the taste of bread and wine with our tongue.[16]

It is Campanella, too, who in the preface to *Metafisica* (1638) opposes a form of knowledge by *tactum intrinsecum in magna suavitate* [inward touch of great sweetness] to reason, 'that is almost an arrow through which we reach towards a faraway target without tasting it (*absque gustu*).' The idea of another form of cognition, as distinct from sensation as science and located between pleasure and knowledge, is the dominant trait of the first definitions of taste as a judgement on the beautiful. All aspects of the problem are contained in a passage from Lodovico Zuccolo's *Discorso delle ragioni del numero del verso italiano* (1623), in which he writes on the beauty of verse:

TASTE

For reasons that cannot be explained by the human mind, this cause is good, since it is in proportion or harmonious, and another bad. In attempting to attribute such a judgement to a certain portion of the intellect that we can know together with the other sensations, we can only seize on the name of a sense. Thus it is that we habitually say the eye discerns the beauty of Painting, and the ear apprehends the harmony of Music. Though truly neither eyes nor ears are judges by themselves, for in this manner even horses and dogs would have that taste for Painting and Music that we enjoy. However, if indeed a certain superior power together with the eye and the ear form such a judgement, such a power we would know only in proportion to

GIORGIO AGAMBEN

our native acuity or expertise in the arts—yet without the use of discourse. The human mind knows well that one body, in order to be beautiful, must be more proportional than another. However, that this is good and that is bad remains entirely the judgement of this power together with the senses, which again we discern without discourse. Wherefore we correctly say, for example, that the mouth should have sufficient outline, angles, opening, lip-size, delicately exposed to the outside in order to respond to the measure and proportion of the nose, the cheeks, the eyes, the brow. It is for this reason that Lucretius had a beautiful mouth, and Camilla an ugly one: yet, because it could be made in one way as much as another, it is of taste, and sensibility remains the judge, understood in the manner above. Thus it would be folly to seek another reason.[17]

This negative characterization, so to speak, of taste as 'knowledge that is not known' is perfectly evident in G. W. Leibniz. Consider his definition of taste ('Taste as distinct from intellect consists in confused perceptions that we cannot sufficiently clarify. It is something close to an instinct.'[18]) in addition to his observation that painters and other artists can judge works of art rather well, yet cannot account for their judgements without recourse to an '*I know not what*' (he writes in *De cognitione, veritate et ideis* [1684]: 'we sometimes see painters and other artists correctly judge what has been done well or done badly; yet they are often unable to give a reason for their judgment but tell the inquirer that the work which displeases them lacks "something, I know not what"'[19]).

Nonetheless, it is precisely this empty sense that in the course of the eighteenth century acquires an ever-more crucial place in intellectual debates. If one were to pick the incomplete article that Montesquieu wrote for the *Encyclopédie* as a paradigmatic example of the numerous sixteenth-century treatises on taste, they would find that, with his usual acumen, he gathered the two essential characteristics of this other knowledge: 'Natural taste is not a theoretical science; it is the quick and exquisite application of rules that one never knows.'[20] 'Taste,' he affirms elsewhere, 'is nothing else but the prerogative to discover, with finesse and alacrity, the magnitude of the pleasure that everything should give to man.'[21] He insists many times on these

TASTE

characteristics which make taste something like the knowledge of pleasure and the pleasure of knowledge. In a significant passage alluding to the arbitrary character of man's constitution ('Our manner of being is entirely arbitrary; we could have been made as we were, or differently. But if we had been made differently, we would sense differently'[22]), he suggests that if the soul were not united with the body, knowledge and pleasure would not be divided: 'If our soul had not been united with a body, it appears that it would have loved what it had knowledge of; in our present state, we love almost only what we do not know.'[23]

From this perspective, taste appears as an excessive sense that cannot find its place within the metaphysical partition between the sensible and the intelligible —yet whose excess defines the particular stature of

GIORGIO AGAMBEN

human knowledge. It is for this reason that philosophers who attempt to describe taste find themselves in the situation of that imaginary traveller in Cyrano de Bergerac's *A Voyage to the Moon* (1649), in which an inhabitant of the moon attempts to explain what he perceives through his senses:

> There are a Million of things, perhaps, in the Universe, that would require a Million of different Organs for your to understand them . . . should I attempt to explain to you what I perceive by the Senses which you want, you would represent it to your self as something that may be Heard, Seen, Felt, Smelt or Tasted, and yet it is no such thing.[24]

TASTE

Taste is precisely such a missing (or excessive) sense that can only be described through metaphor. It is a properly anti-metaphysical sense that permits what is, by definition, impossible: the knowledge of sensible appearances (of the beautiful as 'that which is most apparent') as true and the perception of truth as appearance and pleasure.

Let us now examine the other face of this excessive sense: the beautiful which constitutes its object. In seventeenth- and eighteenth-century treatises we find the latter constituted, in a perfectly symmetrical manner to the concept of taste, as an excessive signifier that can neither be adequately perceived by any sense nor produce any knowledge. The theory of an *I know not what*, having dominated debate over the beautiful since the second half of the seventeenth century, constitutes

GIORGIO AGAMBEN

the point of convergence between the doctrine of the good and that of taste. Father Feijóo wrote in *El no se qué* [I Know Not What] (1733):

> In many of the products not only of nature but also of art (and perhaps art more than nature), men find, instead of those perfections that are the object of their rational comprehension, another genre of mysterious excellence that while flattering their taste, torments their intellect. Their senses feel it, yet reason cannot make it go away. In seeking to explain the phenomena, one can find neither words nor concepts that correspond with one's impressions and so in order to remove the difficulty, one simply says that there is an 'I know not what' that pleases, enamours, enchants, since it is not possible to

find a more clear explanation of this natural mystery.[25]

We also find that Montesquieu, connecting the 'I know not what' as *invisible charm* to surprise ('Sometimes in a person or in a thing there is an invisible attraction, a natural grace that nobody has the knowledge to define, and that is called an 'I know not what'. It appears to me that this effect is principally founded on surprise.'[26]), finishes with the implicit identification of beauty and pleasure, a relation which he derives from the simple perception of an inadequacy between knowledge and its object. According to Descartes's treatise *Passions of the Soul* (1649), wonder, defined as first among the passions, is nothing but an open passion that has no other content than the perception of a split as well as of a difference between an object and our knowledge:

> When our first encounter with some object surprises us and we find it novel, or very different from what we formerly knew or from what we supposed it ought to be, this causes us to wonder and to be astonished at it. Since all this may happen before we know whether or not the object is beneficial to us, I regard wonder as the first of all the passions. It has no opposite, for, if the object before us has no characteristics that surprise us, we are not moved by it at all and we consider it without passion.[27]

In this way the beautiful, as object of taste, comes to ever-more resemble the object of surprise that Descartes defined in a significant expression as a *free cause*: an open object or a pure signifier that no signified has yet to fill.

In an article on the beautiful that Diderot wrote for the *Encyclopédie*, the purification and emptying of the idea of beauty of any possible content is carried to its limit. Here, Diderot defines the beautiful as 'all that excites in my mind the idea of relation'.[28] This idea of relation does not refer, however, to any content or to a precise signified ('When I say everything that awakens in us the idea of relation, I do not mean that, in order to call a being beautiful, we must appreciate what kind of relations there are within it'[29]), nor does it recall in any sense the idea of proportion from classical aesthetics: it is nothing but the pure idea of relation in-itself and for-itself, the pure reference of one thing to another. In other words, relation designates an object's character as signifier, *independent of whatever concrete signified*, which Diderot can, not by chance, exemplify with the parental relation—that is, with something that introduces the individual into a series of purely formal signifying relationships.

> A relation in general is an operation of the understanding, which considers either a being, or a quality, as this being or quality supposes the existence of another being or of another quality. For example: when I say that Peter is a good father, I consider within him a quality that supposes the existence of another, that of a son; so on with other relations, whatever they might be.[30]

TASTE

Through an audacious anthropological excursus, Diderot draws the origin of the idea of relation (and, therefore, that of the beautiful) back towards the problem of the origin and the development of human knowledge qua capacity to perceive signification:

> But the exercise of our intellectual faculties and the necessity to satisfy our needs with inventions, machines, etc., barely had time to sketch notions of order, relation, proportion, arrangement, and symmetry, before we found ourselves among beings where the same notions were, so to speak, iterated ad infinitum; we could not take one step in the universe without awakening these notions; they could enter our souls from anywhere, at any time.[31]

GIORGIO AGAMBEN

Analogous to the manner in which Diderot defines the beautiful as an excessive signifier (and, implicitly, taste as the sense of signification), Rousseau in 'Essay on the Origin of Languages' (1781) separates within our sensations and perceptions the manner in which they conform to the physical actions of objects on our senses, from their power as signs. He, too, attributes the pleasure that is caused by the beautiful exclusively to this second aspect:

> Man is modified by his senses, no one doubts it; but because we fail to distinguish their modifications, we confound their causes; we attribute both too much and too little dominion to sensations; we do not see that often they affect us not only as sensations, but as signs or images.[32]

[...]

TASTE

As long as one wants to consider sounds only in terms of the disturbance they excite in our nerves, one will not have the true principles of music and its power over our hearts. The sounds of a melody do not act on us solely as sounds, but as signs . . . Let whoever wishes to philosophize about the strength of sensations therefore begin by setting aside purely sensual impressions apart from the intellectual and moral impressions which we receive by way of the senses, but of which the senses are only the occasional causes . . . Colours and sounds are capable of a great deal as representations or signs, of little as simple objects of the senses.[33]

In its most radical formulation, eighteenth-century reflection on the beautiful and taste culminates in the return to *knowledge* that one cannot explain since it is grounded on a pure signifier (*Unbezeichnung*, 'absence of signified', as Johann Joachim Winckelmann [1717–68] will define beauty); and to a *pleasure* that allows one to judge since it is sustained not on a substantial reality but, rather, on that which in the object is pure signification.

4. Excessive Knowledge

It is in Kant's *Critique of the Power of Judgement* (1790) that the conception of the beautiful as an excessive signifier as well as of taste as the knowledge and enjoyment of this signifier find their most rigorous expression. From the first page, Kant in fact defines aesthetic pleasure as an excess of representation over knowledge:

> However, the subjective aspect in a representation which cannot become an element of

knowledge at all is the pleasure or displeasure connected with it; for through this I cognize nothing in the object of the representation . . . If pleasure is connected with the mere apprehension (*apprehensio*) of the form of an object of intuition without a relation of this to a concept for a determinate cognition, then the representation is thereby related not to the object, but solely to the subject, and the pleasure can express nothing but its suitability to the cognitive faculties that are in play in the reflecting power of judgement, insofar as they are in play, and thus merely a subjective formal purposiveness of the object . . . That object the form of which (not the material aspect of its representation, as sensation) in mere reflection on it (without any intention of acquiring a concept from it) is judged as the ground of a pleasure in the representation of such an object—with its representation this pleasure is also judged to be necessarily combined, consequently not merely for the subject who apprehends this form but for everyone who judges at all. The object is then called beautiful; and the faculty for judging through such a pleasure (consequently also with universal validity) is called taste.[34]

Readers have often been prevented by the perspective of traditional aesthetics, which finds taste to be a form of knowledge close to logic, from seeing what Kant affirms here with absolute clarity: the beautiful is an excess of representation over knowledge and it is proper that this excess present itself as pleasure. For this reason, Kant does not appear to give the judgement of taste a precise position in the tri-partition of the faculties of the soul ('We can trace all faculties of the human mind without exception back to these three: the faculty of cognition, the feeling of pleasure and displeasure, and the faculty of desire'[35]), but, on the contrary, affirms that it 'reveals an immediate relation between the faculty of cognition with the feeling of pleasure or displeasure' and that this relation is 'precisely what is puzzling in the principle of the faculty of judgement'.[36] That is, on the one hand the judgement of taste is an excess of knowledge that is not known (a 'judgement with which one does not know anything'), but that presents itself as pleasure. On the other hand, it is an excess of pleasure that is not enjoyed ('the universal communicability of a pleasure', Kant writes, 'already includes in its concept that the pleasure itself must not be enjoyed'[37]), but that presents itself as knowledge. Yet, it

GIORGIO AGAMBEN

is in virtue of this fundamentally hybrid situation that taste is the medium term that 'effects the transition from the pure faculty of knowledge, which is to say, from the domain of the concepts of nature, to the domain of the concept of freedom; just as in its logical use, it makes possible the passage from understanding to reason.'[38] For Kant, this hybrid status of taste corresponds just as much with the fact that the beautiful can only be defined through a series of purely negative determinations (*pleasure without interest; universality without concept; finality without end*), as with the impossibility of resolving the antinomy of taste in a convincing fashion. It is the latter antinomy that, in the second section of the *Critique of the Power of Judgement*, he formulates in the following manner:

THESIS: The judgement of taste is not based on concepts, for otherwise it would be possible to dispute about it (decide by means of proofs).

ANTITHESIS: The judgement of taste is based on concepts, for otherwise, despite its variety, it would not even be possible to argue about it (to lay claim to the necessary assent of others to this judgement).[39]

Yet the attempt to resolve this antinomy by placing a 'concept with which one does not know anything' at the foundation of aesthetic judgement is unsatisfactory, as demonstrated by the fact that Kant himself was constrained to return to a 'supersensible' ground and to ultimately admit that the source of judgements of taste remains unknown:

GIORGIO AGAMBEN

Now all contradiction vanishes if I say that the judgement of taste is based on a concept (of a general ground for the subjective purposiveness of nature for the power of judgement), from which, however, nothing can be cognized and proved with regard to the object, because it is in itself indeterminable and unfit for knowledge; yet at the same time by means of this very concept it acquires validity for everyone (in each case, to be sure, as a singular judgement immediately accompanying the intuition), because its determining ground may lie in the concept of that which can be regarded as the supersensible substratum of humanity ... The subjective principle, namely, the indeterminate idea of the supersensible in us, can only be indicated as the sole key to demystifying this faculty which is hidden to us even in its sources, but there is nothing by which it can be made more comprehensible.[40]

Kant clarifies the character of this aesthetic Idea, defining it once again as an excessive image—that is, a representation—which cannot be saved through a concept, just as those constellations that embellish the skies cannot be saved in the Platonic *episteme*:

> As in the case of an Idea of reason the imagination, with its intuitions, never attains to the given concept, so in the case of an aesthetic Idea the understanding, by means of its concepts, never attains to the complete inner intuition of the imagination which it combines with a given representation. Now since to bring a representation of the imagination to concepts is the same

as to expound it, the aesthetic Idea can be called an inexponible representation of the imagination (in its free play).[41]

In Kant's passage, we find again in all its mystery the original Platonic foundation of the Idea through the difference-unity of beauty and truth. As with the Platonic Idea, so too the Kantian aesthetic Idea is entirely contained in the play between a possibility and impossibility of sight (of imagination), between a possibility and impossibility of knowledge. The Idea is a concept that cannot be represented or an image that cannot be expounded. The excess of imagination over understanding grounds beauty (the aesthetic Idea), just as the excess of the concept over the image grounds the domain of the supersensible (the Idea of reason).

TASTE

For this reason, at the end of the second section of the first part of the *Critique of the Power of Judgement*, the beautiful is presented as a 'symbol of morality' and the judgement of taste refers 'to something that is in the subject itself and outside of it, that is neither nature nor freedom, but which is connected with the ground of the latter, namely the supersensible, in which the theoretical faculty is combined with the practical, in a mutual and unknown way, to form a unity'.[42] In establishing such a relationship between taste and the supersensible, Kant carries out the Platonic project to 'save the phenomena' once again.

Yet, in opposition to the discipline of aesthetics, which we find defined in these same years as a *scientia cognitionis sensitivae*, the stature of the Kantian Idea excludes (as with Plato) any possibility for a science of the beautiful:

> There is neither a science of the beautiful, only a critique, nor beautiful science, only beautiful art. For if the former existed, then it would be determined in it scientifically, that is, by means of proofs, whether something should be held to be beautiful or not; thus the judgement about beauty, if it belonged to a science, would not be a judgement of taste. As for the second, a science which, as such, is supposed to be beautiful, is absurd. For if in it, as a science, one were to ask for grounds and proofs, one would be sent packing with tasteful expressions (*bons mots*).[43]

5. Beyond the Subject of Knowledge

In the preceding pages, we have interrogated the concept of taste as the figure through which Western culture has established an ideal of knowledge that it presents as the fullest knowledge at the same time as it underlines the impossibility thereof. Such knowledge, which could suture the metaphysical scission between the sensible and the intelligible, the subject does not in fact know since he cannot explain it. Taste is an empty or excessive sense, situated at the very limit of knowledge and pleasure (from which derives its metaphorical designation as the most opaque sense), whose lack or excess essentially defines the stature of both science (understood as knowledge that is known, can be explained and, therefore, can be learnt and transmitted) and pleasure (understood as a possession on which one cannot found any knowledge).

GIORGIO AGAMBEN

The object and ground of this knowledge that the subject does not know is designated as beauty: something that, according to the Platonic conception, is given to sight (*to kallos*, 'the beautiful', is the most apparent thing, *ekphanestaton*), but of which there can be no science, only love. It was indeed this experience of the impossibility of grasping the object of vision as such (of 'saving the phenomenon') that drove Plato to account for the ideal of knowledge not as 'wisdom' [*sapere*] in the etymological sense (*sophia*) but as the desire for wisdom (*philo-sophia*). That there is beauty, that the phenomena exceed science, is equivalent to saying: there is knowledge that the subject does not know but can only desire or, rather, there is a subject of desire (a *philosophos*) but not a subject of wisdom (a *sophos*). Plato's entire theory of Eros is precisely aimed at bridging these two divided subjects.

TASTE

It is for this reason that Plato was able to connect the knowledge of love [*sapere d'amore*] to divinization. The latter presupposes a knowledge hidden in signs that cannot be known but only recognized: 'this signifies that' (which the most ancient divinatory texts explain as the pure grammatical relationship between a protasis and an apodosis: 'if . . . then . . . '), without any subject of such knowledge, nor it having any other significance than the recognition that 'there is a signifier' or even that 'there is signification'. Indeed, what the diviner knows is only that there is a knowledge that he does not know, from which derives its association with *mania* and possession. It is this very knowledge that Socrates adapts by locating in a 'non-knowledge' the content of knowledge proper and placing in a *daimon*—that is, in the 'other' par excellence—the subject of the knowledge that he professes (in the Cratylus, the word *daimon* is connected

GIORGIO AGAMBEN

with *daemon*, 'he who knows'). The ultimate question posed by the beautiful (and taste as 'knowledge of the beautiful') is, therefore, a question of the subject of knowledge: Who is the subject of knowledge? Who knows?

In the course of this study, while explaining the ideas formulated by seventeenth- and eighteenth-century theorists of the beautiful and taste (Diderot in particular), we have frequently made use of the expression 'excessive signifier'. This expression is derived from an epistemological theory that was first elaborated in the domain of anthropology, but whose relevance for reflection on aesthetics did not escape its author: here we refer to the theory of signification that Levi-Strauss developed through the concept of *mana* in *Introduction to the Work of Marcel Mauss* (1950).

TASTE

As is well known, Levi-Strauss posited a fundamentally inadequate relation between signification and knowledge that translates to an irreducible excess of the signifier over the signified, the cause of which is inscribed in the origin of man as *Homo sapiens*:

> Things cannot have begun to signify gradually. In the wake of a transformation which is not a subject of study for the social sciences, but for biology and psychology, a shift occurred from a stage when nothing had a meaning to another stage when everything had meaning. Actually, that apparently banal remark is important, because that radical change has no counterpart in the field of knowledge, which develops slowly and progressively. In other words, at the moment when the entire universe all at once

GIORGIO AGAMBEN

became *significant*, it was none the better *known* for being so, even if it is true that the emergence of language must have hastened the rhythm of the development of knowledge. So there is a fundamental opposition, in the history of the human mind, between symbolism which is characteristically discontinuous, and knowledge, characterized by continuity. Let us consider what follows from that. It follows that the two categories of the signifier and the signified came to be constituted simultaneously and interdependently, as complementary units; whereas knowledge, that is, the intellectual process which enables us to identify certain aspects of the signifier and certain aspects of the signified, one with reference to the other—we could even say the process which enables us to choose, from the

TASTE

entirety of the signifier and from the entirety of the signified, those parts which present the most satisfying relations of mutual agreement—only got started very slowly. It is as if humankind had suddenly acquired an immense domain and the detailed plan of that domain along with a notion of the reciprocal relationship of domain and plan; but had spent millennia learning which specific symbols of the plan represented the different aspects of the domain. The universe signified long before people began to know what it signified; no doubt that goes without saying. But, from the foregoing analysis, it also emerges that from the beginning, the universe signified the totality of what humankind can expect to know about it. What people call the progress of the human mind and, in any case, the progress of scientific knowledge, could only have been and can only ever be constituted out of processes of correcting and recutting of patterns, regrouping, defining relationships of belonging and discovering new resources, inside a totality which is closed and complementary to itself. [. . .]

We can therefore expect the relationship between symbolism and knowledge to conserve common features in the non-industrial societies and in our own, although those features would not be equally pronounced in the two types of society. It does not mean that we are creating a gulf between them, if we acknowledge that the work of equalizing of the signifier to fit the signified has been pursued more methodically and rigorously from the time when modern science was born, and within the boundaries of the spread of science. But everywhere else, and still constantly in our own societies (and no doubt for a long time to come), a fundamental situation perseveres which arises out of the human condition: namely, that man has from the start had at his disposition a signifier-totality which he is at a loss to know how to allocate to a signified, given as such, but no less unknown for being given. There is always a non-equivalence or 'inadequation' between the two, a non-fit and overspill which divine understanding alone can soak up; this generates a signifier-surfeit relative to the signifieds to which it can be fitted. So, in man's effort to understand the world, he always disposes of a surplus of signification (which he

GIORGIO AGAMBEN

shares out among things in accordance with the laws of the symbolic thinking which it is the task of ethnologists and linguists to study). That distribution of a supplementary ration—if I can express myself thus—is absolutely necessary to ensure that, in total, the available signifier and the mapped-out signified may remain in the relationship of complementarity which is the very condition of the exercise of symbolic thinking.

I believe that notions of the *mana* type, however diverse they may be, and viewed in terms of their most general function (which, as we have seen, has not vanished from our mentality and our form of society) represent nothing more or less than that *floating signifier* which is the disability of all finite thought (but also the surety of all art, all poetry, every mythic and aesthetic invention), even though scientific knowledge is capable, if not of staunching it, at least of controlling it partially.[44]

We can at this point extend Levi-Strauss' considerations to all the epistemological statutes of Western culture, from the ancient world until today. Consider, from this perspective what Plato affirms at the end of Book 7 of the *Republic* with respect to astronomy as *episteme*: that, as we have seen, it is unable to exhaust the visible phenomena as such—those beautiful constellations that embellish the skies—through its explanations but must instead seek the invisible and numeric relations that the former presuppose. We can conclude that ancient science left free in the phenomena what was pure appearance in them (that is, pure signifier), opening beside itself a space that divinatory science could occupy without contradiction.

The example of astronomy and astrology (which peacefully coexisted in antiquity) is clarifying: the first is limited to expounding the movement of the stars and their reciprocal positions, as a manner of 'saving appearances' in the sense that Simplicius gave to this expression—yet without offering any explanation as such of those beautiful figures that the stars trace in the sky. The phenomena 'saved' by science therefore inevitably leave behind a free residue, a pure signifier that astrology can take as its support and treat as a supplement of signification to distribute at its whim.

In the ancient world, there are thus two species of knowledge: knowledge that is known, which is to say science in the modern sense as founded upon the adequation of signifier and signified; and knowledge that is not known, which is to say, divinatory science (and the various forms of *mania* enumerated by Plato) that is conversely founded upon the excessive signifier. Returning to the distinction between *semiotic* and *semantic* that Benveniste has formulated as the 'double signification' inherent in human language, one can define the first as semantic knowledge—that has a subject and can be explained—and the second as semiotic knowledge—that does not have a subject and can only be recognized.[45] Between these two forms of knowledge, Plato placed philosophy which, as *mania*, pertains to divination. However, in perceiving the phenomena as beauty it is not limited to carrying out a distribution of the excessive signifier but, thanks to the mediation of Eros, is able instead to save the phenomena in the Idea.

GIORGIO AGAMBEN

Since the eighteenth century, modern science has extended its territory only at the expense of the divinatory sciences which came to be excluded from knowledge. The subject of science poses itself as the only subject of knowledge, negating the possibility of any knowledge without subject. Nonetheless, the decline of the traditional divinatory sciences did not by any means signal the disappearance of this knowledge that is not known: the growing debate over the '*I know not what*' and taste starting in the seventeenth century and the progressive consolidation of the aesthetic throughout the nineteenth century demonstrates, rather, that science can neither fill nor reduce the excessive signifier. If aesthetics as knowledge of the excessive signifier (of the beautiful) is but a substitute for divination, it is nonetheless not the only knowledge in the modern epoch that comes to the fore after the eclipse of the divinatory

TASTE

sciences. In the course of the nineteenth century, even the philological disciplines grasp their own specificity with respect to the natural sciences, explicitly founding their knowledge and method in a hermeneutic circle of the divinatory variety (which means, if one properly reflects, that the question 'Who knows?' in the reading and interpretation of a text—whether it is the interpreter, the author, or the text itself—is not a question that can easily be answered).

Yet another science—whose formative process chronologically coincides with that of the science of the beautiful and that, since the eighteenth century, has assumed a growing importance within the system of knowledge—reveals an unexpected affinity with aesthetics if taste is indeed as much a knowledge that is not known, as a pleasure that is not enjoyed but judged and measured. We refer, of course, to political economy. Where aesthetics takes as its object a knowledge that is not known, political economy takes as its object a pleasure that is not enjoyed. One could say, in fact, that the latter science begins by identifying its own domain with the 'interested pleasure' that Kant rigorously excluded from the confines of the beautiful. If this is so, are not Marx's teachings but the demonstration (placing the value-form and fetish-character of the commodity at the centre of his analyses in the first chapter of *Capital* [1867]) that this discipline is founded not so much on use value (on utility, an enjoyed pleasure) as it is on exchange value, which is to say, on that which can neither be enjoyed nor grasped in the object—a pleasure that one cannot have? As Georg Simmel intuited in defining money (with an expression that singularly recalls Diderot's definition of the beautiful) as a 'pure relation without content', the value-form, like Levi-Strauss' *mana*, is a zero symbolic value or pure signifier that simply indicates the necessity of a supplementary symbolic content and a supplementary pleasure, whose calculus constitutes the object of economic science.

Mallarmé's observation, according to which aesthetics and political economy are the only paths open to research on the mind [*ricerca mentale*], is thus more than a superficial analogy.[46] Aesthetics and political economy, *Homo æstheticus* and *Homo œconomicus*, are in a certain sense the two halves (a knowledge that is not known and a pleasure that is not enjoyed) that taste struggled to hold together for the last time in the experience of a knowledge that enjoys and a pleasure that knows, before their explosion and liberation helped set in motion those tremendous transformations that essentially characterize modern society.

At the end of the nineteenth century, another science came to occupy the terrain left vacant by divinatory science, a science that—inasmuch as it defines its own domain as the 'unconscious'—was instituted on the assumption that there is a knowledge that is not known, but that is revealed in symbols and signifiers. As written by he who has derived the most extreme and rigorous consequences that were only implicit in the original appearance of psychoanalysis as semiotic knowledge, 'analysis came to announce that there is knowledge that is not known, knowledge that is sustained by the signifier itself . . . the unconscious testifies to knowledge that escapes the speaking being'.[47]

TASTE

While psychoanalysis bears an essential proximity to aesthetics (that the concept of the unconscious appears for the first time in Leibniz at the limits of that *cognitio sensitiva confusa* which aesthetics will define as its proper sphere is certainly a proof of such proximity), its relation with political economy is no less essential. For the *Es*[48] (a third-person pronoun or non-subject according to the linguists) that analysis places as the subject of a knowledge that is not known is also the subject of a pleasure that is not enjoyed. Recognizing the unconscious as the space of libidinal economy, psychoanalysis is situated at the limit between aesthetics and political economy, between a knowledge that is not known and a pleasure that is not enjoyed—and tends to conjoin them in a unitary project. (The idea of an 'aesthetics guided by an economic point of view' that Freud formulates in

GIORGIO AGAMBEN

the second chapter of *Beyond the Pleasure Principle* [1920], is certainly significant).

Despite assisting an unprecedented consolidation of the natural sciences, modern culture has also helped in various ways to constitute and reinforce the new semiotic science that takes as its object a knowledge that is not known and a pleasure that is not enjoyed. The importance of the excessive signifier not only does not diminish, but, in a certain sense, expands. It is almost as if the more that science progresses in its attempt to 'save appearances', the greater becomes that residue of the excessive signifier (the quantity of knowledge that is not known) that must be examined by the divinatory sciences. Semiotic science and semantic science, divination and science strictly appear together linked through a relation of complementarity, in which the one guarantees the possibility and the function of the other.

TASTE

The fracture between signification and knowledge —the semiotic and the semantic—is not in fact something produced once and for all outside of the human, but instead is a fracture of this very same subject of knowledge: man as *Homo sapiens*. Since, as a speaking and thinking being, the human is held between signification and knowledge, its cognition is necessarily split and the problem of who knows knowledge (the problem of the subject of knowledge) remains the fundamental question of every epistemology. Despite proceeding from the most profound intentions of ancient philosophy (as of Spinoza's *Ethics*) in assuming the Idea (or God) to be the principle of knowledge, philosophy and modern science since Descartes have instead sought to guarantee the unity of cognition through the fiction of an *ego cogito*, the *I* as pure self-consciousness, affirmed as the only subject of knowledge. Yet it is this very subject of knowledge that the most recent developments in the human sciences have called into question. For example, consider psychoanalysis, which has discovered *Es* to be the subject of a knowledge that is not known; as well as structuralism, which has established structure to be an unconscious categorical knowledge without reference to any thinking subject; and linguistics, which has located in the phoneme a knowledge independent of the speaking subject—all resolutely signal towards an Other as the subject of knowledge. At this point, the problem becomes that of the passage between the knowledge that is known and the knowledge that is not known, between knowledge of the Other and knowledge of the subject. Yet, as Benveniste has demonstrated that the semiotic and semantic in language represent two closed worlds between which there is no passage, so there is a hiatus

TASTE

between knowledge of the Other and knowledge of the subject that cannot clearly be bridged. The Freudian program—according to which 'where *Es* was, the I should be'—cannot be realized if it is true that the I and the Other are in fact a necessary pair.

It is perhaps not surprising, then, that modern humanity continues to be ever less capable of mastering a knowledge and a pleasure that, to an increasing extent, do not belong to it. Between knowledge of the subject and knowledge without subject, between the I and the Other, an abyss has opened that technology and economy seek in vain to bridge.

Hence, too, semiotics' incapacity to constitute itself as a general science of the sign, that is, as a knowledge founded upon the unity of signifier and signified. In order to constitute itself as such, it would have to both reduce the signifier's excess and suture the scission between semiotic knowledge and semantic knowledge, between a knowledge that is not known and a knowledge that is known—a scission which is inscribed in the very notion of the sign on which the discipline is founded. For this reason, one can view the case of Saussure's studies on Saturnian verses—so embarrassing to the linguists—as paradigmatic of semiology's destiny: semiology, having recognized that there is a knowledge of signifiers that is not known yet that reveals itself in anagrams, cannot but seek to attribute this to a subject that can never be found for the simple reason that it has never been.[49] A knowledge that would neither be semiotic knowledge nor semantic knowledge— or that would be both at the same time—could not but situate itself in that fracture between signifier and

TASTE

signified that semiology has, so far, always tried to eliminate and obscure.

It is perhaps at this point that we are able to grasp the sense of the Greek project for a *philo-sophia*, for a love of knowledge and a knowledge of love, that would be neither knowledge of the signifier nor knowledge of the signified, neither divination nor science, neither knowledge nor pleasure. So, too, may we now grasp that the concept of taste constitutes an extreme and late incarnation of this very project. For only a knowledge that does not belong either to the subject or the Other but instead is situated in the fracture that divides them can claim to have truly 'saved the phenomena' in their pure appearance, without either referring them back to being and an invisible truth or abandoning them to divination as an excessive signifier.

GIORGIO AGAMBEN

It is this knowledge in which truth and beauty communicate that, at the culmination of Greek philosophy, Plato fixed in the demonic figure of Eros. It is also this knowledge that, at the threshold of the modern age, appeared to the poets of the Duecento as the 'understanding of love' in the beatified figure of a Woman (Beatrice) in whom, finally, science enjoys and pleasure knows. The mythologem of Eros is necessarily inscribed in the destiny of Western philosophy inasmuch as, beyond the metaphysical diremption of signifier and signified, appearance and being, as well as divination and science, it strives towards an integral salvation of the phenomena. Knowledge of love, philosophy, signifies: beauty must save truth and truth must save beauty. In this double salvation, knowledge is realized.

TASTE

Only such a pleasure, in which pleasure and knowledge are united, could attain to the ideal of wisdom [*sapienzale*] and thus taste that an Indian poetic treatise, *The Mirror of Composition* (*Sahitya-darpana*), has fixed in the concept of 'flavour' [*sapore*] (*rasa*):

> Arising from a luminous principle, indivisible, resplendent in its self-evidence, made of joy and thought together, free of contact with any other perceptions, twin to the savouring of the *brahman*, living on the breath of supernatural marvel, such is the Flavour that those who have the means of judgement enjoy as the proper form of self, inseparably.[50]

NOTES

1 Aristotle, 'Nicomachean Ethics' in *The Complete Works of Aristotle*, VOL. 2 (Jonathan Barnes ed.) (Princeton: Princeton University Press, 1984), 1118a.

2 G. W. F. Hegel, *Ästhetik* (Berlin: Aufbau-Verlag, 1955), p. 696.

NOTES

3 Saint Isidoro of Sevilla, *Las Etimologías* [The Etymologies], VOL. 10 (Madrid: Biblioteca de Autores Cristianos, 2004), p. 240.

4 Friedrich Nietzsche, 'Die vorplatonische Philosophen' [The Pre-Platonic Philosophers] in *Gesammelte Werke*, VOL. 4 (München: Musarion Verlag, 1921), pp. 253–4.

5 Immanuel Kant, *Critique of the Power of Judgement* (Paul Guyer ed., Paul Guyer and Eric Matthews trans) (Cambridge: Cambridge University Press, 2002), p. 57.

6 Montesquieu, 'Gusto' in *Enciclopedia o dizionario ragionato delle scienze, delle arti e dei mestieri* [Encyclopedia, or a Systematic Dictionary of the Sciences, Arts and Crafts] (Paolo Casini ed.) (Bari: Laterza, 1968), p. 735.

7 Plato, *Phaedrus*, in *Plato in Twelve Volumes*, VOL. 9 (Harold N. Fowler trans.) (Cambridge: Harvard University Press, 1925), 250d.

8 Plato, *Symposium*, in *Plato in Twelve Volumes*, VOL. 9 (Harold N. Fowler trans.) (Cambridge: Harvard University Press, 1925), 202a.

9 Ibid. 204a–b.

10 Ibid. 211a–b.

11 Plato, *Republic*, in *Plato in Twelve Volumes*, VOLS 5 and 6 (Harold N. Fowler trans.) (Cambridge: Harvard University Press, 1925), 529c–2.

12 Pierre Duhem, *Sozein ta Phainomena: Essai sur la notion de théorie physique de Platon à Galilée* [To Save the Phenomena: An Essay on the Idea of Physical

NOTES

Theory from Plato to Galileo] (Paris: Hermann, 1908), p. 3.

13 Plato, *Symposium*, 204d.

14 Plato, *Philebus*, in *Plato in Twelve Volumes,* VOL. 9 (Harold N. Fowler trans.) (Cambridge: Harvard University Press, 1925), 64e.

15 Robert Klein, '"Giudizio" and "Gusto" dans la théorie de l'art au Cinquecento' ["Judgement" and "Taste" in Cinquecento Art Theory] in *La forme et l'intelligible: écrits sur la Renaissance et l'art modern* (André Chastel ed.) (Paris: Gallimard, 1970).

16 Ibid, p. 377.

17 Lodovico Zuccolo, *Discorso delle ragioni del numero del verso italiano* [Discourse on the Reasons for the Meter

NOTES

of Italian Verse] (Venice: Appresso Marco Ginami, 1623). pp. 8–9.

18 G. W. Leibniz as quoted in V. E. Alfieri, *L'estetica dall'illuminismo al romanticismo fuori di Italia* [Aesthetics Outside Italy from the Enlightenment to Romanticism], in *Momenti e problemi di storia dell' estetica*, VOL. 3 (Milan: Marzatori, 1959), p. 631.

19 G. W. Leibniz, 'Meditations on Knowledge, Truth and Ideas' in *Philosophical Papers and Letters*, VOL. 1 (Leroy E. Loemker ed.) (Chicago: University of Chicago Press, 1956), p.449.

20 Montesquieu, 'Gusto', p. 735.

21 Ibid., p.734.

22 Ibid.

23 Ibid.

24 Cyrano de Bergerac, *A Voyage to the Moon* (New York: Doubleday and McClure Co, 1899), p. 85–6.

25 Father Feijóo as quoted in Benedetto Croce, *Estetica come scienza dell'espressione e linguistica generale* (Bari: Laterza, 1950), p. 226. [Available in Spanish: https://goo.gl/ZmTTvg (last accessed on 19 June 2017).]

26 Montesquieu, 'Gusto', p.745.

27 René Descartes, 'The Passions of the Soul' in *The Philosophical Writings of Descartes*, VOL. 1 (John Cottingham, Robert Stoothoff , Dugald Murdoch trans) (Cambridge: Cambridge University Press, 1985). p. 350.

NOTES

28 Denis Diderot, 'Beautiful' in *The Encyclopedia of Diderot and d'Alembert Collaborative Translation Project* (Philippe Bonin trans.) (Ann Arbor: University of Michigan Library, 2006). [Available at: https://goo.gl/RwA5CC (last accessed on 25 April 2017).]

29 Ibid.

30 Ibid.

31 Ibid.

32 Jean-Jacques Rousseau, *Essay on the Origin of Languages and Writings Related to Music* (John Scott ed. and trans.) (Hanover: University Press of New England, 1998), p. 319.

33 Ibid., pp. 323–4.

34 Kant, *Critique of the Power of Judgement*, pp. 75–6.

NOTES

35 Ibid., p. 11.

36 Ibid., p. 57.

37 Ibid., p. 185.

38 Ibid., p. 66.

39 Ibid., p. 215.

40 Ibid., pp. 216–17.

41 Ibid., p. 219.

42 Ibid., p. 227.

43 Ibid., p. 184.

44 Claude Levi-Strauss, *Introduction to the Work of Marcel Mauss* (Felicity Baker trans.) (London: Routledge, 1970), pp. 59–63.

45 Emile Benveniste, *Problèmes de linguistique générale* [Problems in General Linguistics], VOL. 2 (Paris: Gallimard, 1974).

46 Stéphane Mallarmé, 'Magie' in *Divagations* (Paris: Fasquelle, 1897), p. 322.

47 Jacques Lacan, *Le seminaire. Livre XX: Encore* (Paris: Seuil, 1975), p. 88.

48 In the context of psychoanalysis, the conventional English translation of '*Es*' is the term 'Id'. However, the original '*Es*' is not a neologism but simply the third-person pronoun 'it', to which Agamben refers here. [Trans.]

49 Jean-Claude Milner, *L'amour de la langue* [For the Love of Language] (Paris: Seuil, 1978).

NOTES

50 René Daumal, *I poteri della parola* [The Powers of the Word] (Claudio Rugafiori ed.) (Milano: Adelphi, 1968), p. 165.